CH01263229

NEXT PLANE TO LONDON

NEXT PLANE TO LONDON

BRYCE BLACKHEART

FISHBONE
IMPRINTS

This is a work of fiction. Names, characters, places, and incidents either are the product of the author's imagination or are used fictitiously. Any resemblance to actual persons, living or dead, events, or locales is entirely coincidental.

NEXT PLANE TO LONDON. Copyright © 2024 by Bryce Blackheart. All rights reserved. Published in the United States by Fishbone Imprints.

www.fishboneimprints.com

No part of this publication may be reproduced, distributed, or transmitted in any form or by any means, including photocopying, recording, or other electronic or mechanical methods, without the prior written permission of the publisher, except as permitted by U.S. copyright law. For permission requests contact fishboneimprints.com.

Publisher's Cataloging-in-Publication data

Names: Blackheart, Bryce, author.

Title: Next plane to London / Bryce Blackheart.

Description: Mentor, OH: Fishbone Imprints, 2024. Identifiers: LCCN: 2024915861 | ISBN: 979-8-9912274-2-1 (hardcover) | 979-8-9912274-1-4 (paperback) | 979-8-9912274-0-7 (ebook) | 979-8-9912274-3-8 (audio) Subjects: LCSH Missing persons--Fiction. | Family--Fiction. | Dysfunctional families--Fiction. | Mystery fiction. | Thriller fiction. | BISAC FICTION / Thrillers / Suspense | FICTION / Mystery & Detective / General | FICTION / Mystery & Detective / Women Sleuths Classification: LCC PS3602 .L33 N49 2024 | DDC 813.6--dc23

First Edition: October 2024

Dedicated to my Mother

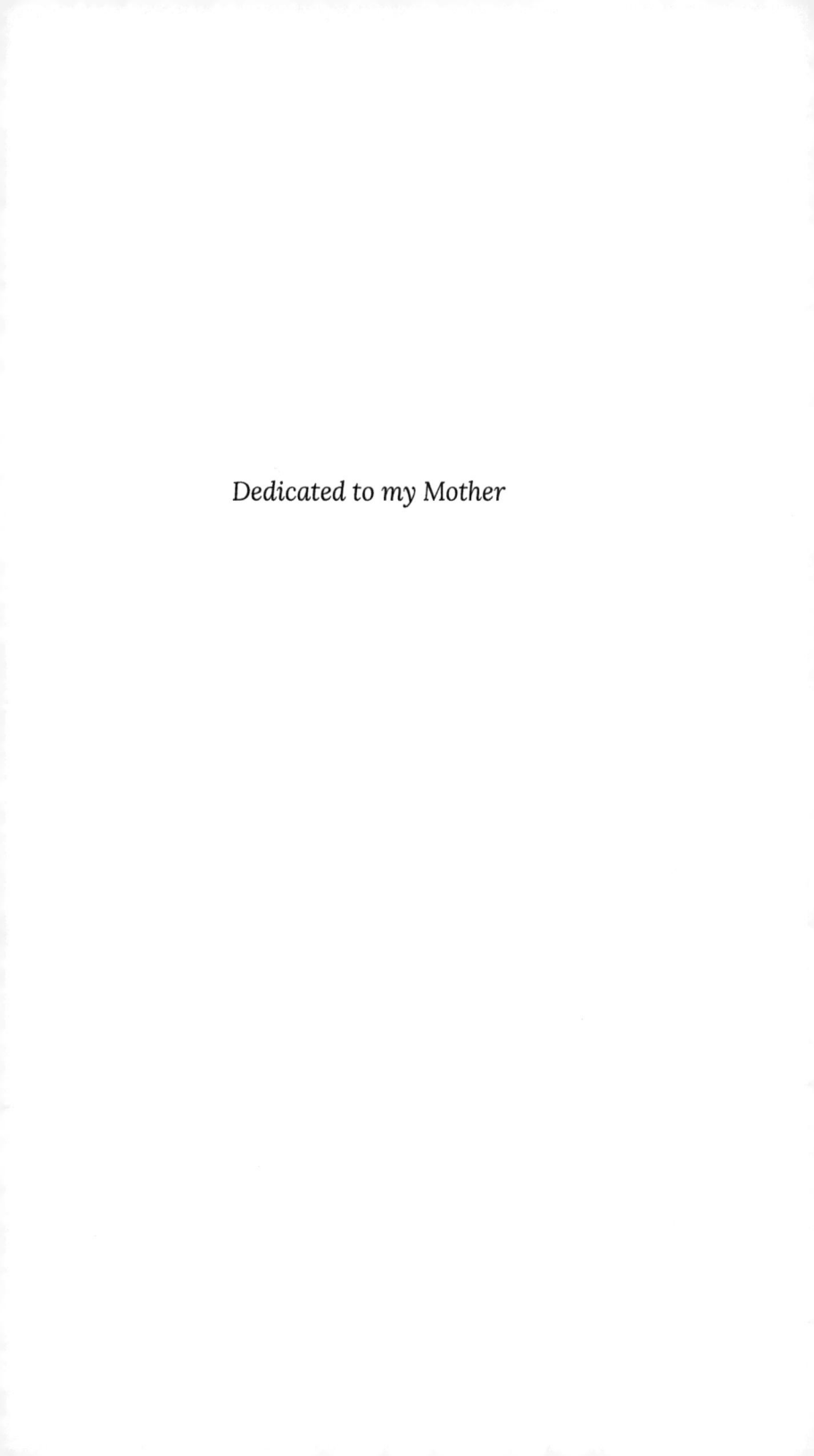

Part One

Chapter 1

Ella jolted awake sharply, momentarily disoriented by her surroundings. She was back in her childhood bedroom in Bay Ridge, Brooklyn. Her cat, Iris, was nestled beside her, rumbling soft purrs. But Ella felt anything but at peace, the lingering remnants of her nightmare still haunting her.

Faded echoes of her twin sibling's frantic and desperate pleas replayed in her mind, his words full of fear and confusion, his voice a jumble of words: "Ella, help me... can't find... I've lost... time." His face appeared so vivid, his eyes urgent and wide. But as she attempted to reach out to him, he slipped just beyond her grasp, his form fading.

It'd been eight days since Oscar disappeared without a trace. The police were running out of leads, their investigation stalled, and she couldn't help but feel that she should be doing more to find him. Her guilt made it hard to breathe, the room already stuffy and full of so many memories of their childhood.

"Morning, Iris," Ella murmured, her voice heavy with sleep and tinged with a melancholy that had become all too familiar. She propped herself on her elbows and ran a hand through her tousled brown hair. After Oscar's disappearance, she put the move to London with her boyfriend on hold in favor of living with her mother,

Adelaide. She had no choice but to stay in Oscar's room—the one they used to share as children.

Ella rubbed her eyes, trying to banish the dream from her mind. She sighed and picked up a photo of Oscar beside the bed, his thick brown hair and bright smile frozen in time. "Where are you?" she whispered. "What do you want to tell me?"

She put the photo back on the nightstand and stroked Iris's fur. "I don't function very well as a human being without my brother." She confessed out loud in a hollow, mocking tone.

Iris just blinked in reply, her green eyes full of feline indifference. Ella swung her legs over the side of the bed, watching as Iris jumped off and meandered around the room, her tail swishing lazily.

Ella followed with slow and deliberate movements, an effort not to wake her mother sleeping down the hall. Adelaide hadn't taken Oscar's disappearance well. She paced the apartment at all hours, her mind consumed by worry and dark thoughts, muttering to herself and jumping at every shadow. Her drinking only exacerbated the situation, and she didn't get much sleep as it stood.

The kitchen was eerily quiet. Once there, the silence was broken only by a soft meow as Iris hopped onto a chair at the kitchen table.

Ella dropped some slices of bread into the toaster and began to make some coffee. Her mind drifted to one of her last conversations with Oscar. They had argued about something insignificant, as siblings often do. Now, she couldn't even remember what it had been about, perhaps a borrowed shirt or a misplaced book. If only she had known that it might be their last.

She took a seat at the table. On the fridge rested a magnet, which was some old thing likely bought on vacation. It held up a photo of her and Oscar, their arms draped around each other, smiles wide and genuine. The contrast between the image and the current reality was a bitter pill. She quickly finished her toast and headed for the living room, the cat pacing right behind.

Ella settled down on the sagging floral-print couch, clutching her coffee mug. The warmth seeped into her palms as she surveyed the living room—once a cozy space, it was now just another artifact of their crumbling lives. She couldn't help but ponder the dream again. *Could it be a sign or a message? What could it possibly mean?*

She was grateful to see him again, even if only in a dream. Dreams can be an escape from the real world, sometimes even the nightmares. She decided to push it aside—*just a dream, nothing more.*

Ella sipped her coffee again. A calendar hung on the hall closet, making it very apparent that her departure date had passed, a bold red circle around October 4th. She imagined Sam alone in London, waiting for her. A pang of guilt twisted in her stomach. They had been so excited to start this new chapter of their lives, to experience the thrill of a new city and the freedom of living with one another.

But then Oscar disappeared, and everything changed.

Ella remembered the frantic phone call from her mother, her voice trembling with panic. "Oscar's gone. He's just... missing. His friends haven't heard from him, and his cell phone is off. It's not like him."

Those words alone shattered Ella's world and tossed her life off course. Adelaide's usually stern voice had been replaced by raw fear, a sound that was very rare from her. Ever since that day, she hasn't been able to imagine a normal life.

How could she leave now with her family broken and lost? How could she leave her mother in this time of unimaginable anguish? Ella knew she had to stay a little longer. She thought about the boxes in her bedroom, packed and ready for the move that never happened. How long would they sit there? They would likely be gathering dust.

Ella's phone buzzed abruptly from the pocket of her pajamas. She fished it out and felt her throat tighten at the name flashing on the screen. Sam.

With a weary sigh, she swiped to answer the call. "Hey." She tried to inject some levity into her tone.

"Ella! Thank God," Sam said, relief evident in his voice. "Have you heard anything? Is there any news?"

"No. Nothing. The police have found nothing. No leads or clues, still just dead ends and... unanswered questions."

Sam's responding sigh crackled across the line. "I'm so sorry. I can't even imagine."

Ella's fingers tightened around her phone as she listened to Sam's sympathetic words. She longed for simpler times when they were still at NYU, where they first met and were inseparable throughout college.

"I wish you were still in New York," Ella reminisced. "Being able just to see you..."

"I do, too. Starting this new job, the timing couldn't be worse. I won't be able to leave London right now, not with everything on my plate. I'm so sorry, Ella."

A wave of frustration washed over her. "I know, I know. I feel so alone here. Everything feels broken. It's hard to think straight without you."

"I wish I could be there to help you cope with this," Sam said earnestly. "We were about to start a new adventure together, and now... it all feels so out of reach. But we will get through it, I promise."

Ella wanted to believe him, but doubt gnawed at her. She twisted a strand of her brown hair around her finger. "I can't help thinking that if you were still here, maybe things would be different. Maybe both of us could have prevented whatever happened to Oscar. Maybe we could have seen the signs if he were in trouble, or... I don't know, done something."

"Who knows? Maybe?" he said softly. "But you're not alone. Even from a distance, I'm still here for you. I'm just a call away, day or night."

Ella sniffed hard, blinking back the resurgence of hot tears. She clutched the phone tighter. "I know, Sammy," she whispered. "Soon. Once we know what's happened to Oscar, any sooner, it wouldn't feel right."

"Right." His voice was thick with concern. "Just promise me you'll take care of yourself?"

Ella's heart swelled with gratitude at his words. "I will, I promise. I should probably get ready for work now; my shift starts soon. I'm filling in for Oscar at the coffeehouse today. Don't want to be late."

"Just remember, I'm always here if you need me. Just keep me updated, okay?"

"Thanks; I really appreciate that."

She hung up and set her phone aside, absently stroking Iris with her free hand, who had curled up beside her during the call.

Ella rummaged through an unpacked suitcase, fingers brushing against familiar fabrics until she found a well-worn black T-shirt and a pair of ripped jeans. She shook her head, trying to stop her mind from racing.

Was Oscar kidnapped? Is he hurt somewhere and desperately needing her help? The police had been helpful but mostly seemed to take a wait-and-see approach.

She reached for her phone on the nightstand, heart skipping beats as she checked for missed calls or messages. Nothing. Just like every day since Oscar disappeared.

Ella slipped the phone into her pocket and looked around the room, taking in the remnants of her brother's life. His guitar leaning against the wall. A stack of books teetering precariously on the desk, their pages full of scribbled notes and song lyrics. Her eyes lingered on more framed photographs of the two of them, always with their arms around each other, grinning at the camera. Such innocent times are now tainted by reality.

Getting ready in the mirror, her red and swollen eyes were all she could focus on. She splashed some cold water on her face and checked her appearance one last time before tying her hair into a ponytail.

Iris snaked between Ella's ankles and meowed insistently. "I know, I know," Ella bent down to scratch behind Iris's ears. "You're hungry."

In the kitchen, Adelaide turned to give Iris a scornful look. The cat shrank back under the withering stare, tucking her tail between her legs and seeking refuge behind Ella's ankles.

"I swear if that mangy beast pees on my rugs..." Adelaide trailed off, shuffling through the kitchen in a ratty pink bathrobe that had seen better days. The harsh light overhead cast unflattering shadows on her face.

Ella grabbed a scoop and filled the cat's food bowl. "Good morning to you too, Mom."

Her mother grunted in response, bloodshot eyes narrowing as she watched Ella tend to the cat. Hints of stale wine and body odor wafted from her mother's unwashed form.

"I guess I ought to be thankful." Adelaide stared at the cat as it cautiously approached its food bowl. "At least the filthy creature might catch some rodents in this godforsaken dump," she gestured at the water-stained ceiling.

Ella knew better than to snap back. Even before Oscar disappeared, antagonizing Adelaide was like poking a semi-feral animal.

"I'm going to work," Ella said dryly as she grabbed her battered jean jacket off the hook and shrugged it on. She paused in the doorway, giving Iris one last affectionate look. "Be good for Mommy, okay?"

A resigned sigh escaped Ella's lips. She closed the apartment door behind her, the click of the lock echoing in the empty hallway.

Trudging to the elevator, her boots scuffed against the threadbare carpet. She jabbed the call button more forcefully than necessary, watching as the numbers above the doors flickered.

"Come on, you piece of shit," she said under her breath, tapping her foot.

The building's elevator was notoriously unreliable, prone to sudden breakdowns and long periods of disrepair. Ella had stopped counting the number of times she'd been forced to take the stairs, legs burning from the effort of climbing seven flights. She glanced at her watch, anxiety creeping in as the seconds ticked by. *Don't be late, don't be late.*

The machinery groaned behind the closed doors as if mocking her urgency. She pressed the button again, harder this time, as if its sheer force would make the elevator car move faster.

The doors finally creaked open to reveal the cramped interior. Ella stepped inside, her nose wrinkling at the stale air that greeted her. Admiring the walls covered in a patchwork of graffiti and scratched initials, she pressed the button for the lobby, sending up a silent prayer that she wouldn't get trapped between floors.

She leaned back against the wall, trying to ignore the elevator's unsettling sway as it descended. Concentrating on her breathing, she willed her racing heart to slow down.

Suddenly, a loud clang echoed through the shaft, and the elevator lurched to a jarring halt. Ella's stomach sank as the lights flickered and then dimmed entirely, leaving her in the dark.

"No, no, no," she muttered, fear rising quickly. She slammed her palm against the call button, but the only response was a faint buzzing sound.

Every second felt like an eternity. She thought of Iris, curled up somewhere, blissfully unaware of her predicament. It was useless to scream for help—her cries would likely be dismissed in a building where strange noises were commonplace.

Just as she began to feel nauseatingly claustrophobic, a low moan echoed through the elevator shaft. It quickly shifted back into motion, almost knocking Ella off balance. All the lights flickered back to life, a harsh fluorescent glow casting stark shadows across the small space. She let out a shaky breath. The elevator slowly resumed its descent.

At once, the doors grinded open to reveal the lobby. Ella practically tumbled out, legs shaking with relief, and she took a breath of the marginally fresher air. She strolled past the battered mailboxes out through the front doors, grateful to see the sidewalk.

The mid-October wind had picked up, whipping through the city streets with a biting chill. She shivered and pulled her jacket tighter around her. Dry leaves scattered around, their crisp rustling drowning out the sound of traffic and pedestrians.

She gazed up at the cloudy sky above the buildings ahead, several gray masses obscuring any hint of sunlight. She could still make out the towering suspension cables of the Verrazano Bridge in the distance...

Thoughts of Oscar grew in her mind before a familiar figure caught her eye, huddled against the side of a dilapidated building and partially obscured by overgrown bushes. It was the old homeless man she often saw on the way to work.

His angular face was etched with furrowed and weathered lines, a roadmap of a long life and hardships endured. Dirty, tattered clothes hung loosely from his frail frame, and a filthy blanket covered his lap.

Usually, she would have moved on without a second glance. Today, something compelled her to slow down, captivated by an inexplicable force.

As she approached without much thought, the man lifted his head and fixed her with a stare that pierced her soul. His eyes were a startling blue, clear and sharp despite his age.

"Spare some change, miss?" he rasped, extending a gnarled hand toward her.

Ella shook her head, averting her eyes. "Sorry, I don't have any cash on me right now."

She started to continue walking by, but the man's words cut through the air like a blade.

"He's sorry he had to leave you." His voice took on a strange, distant quality. "He didn't mean to leave you like this."

Ella's heart stuttered in her chest, and a cold sweat broke out on her skin. She whirled around to face the man, her eyes wild.

"What did you say?"

The man tilted his head, a sad smile tugging at the edges of his cracked lips. "He's sorry he had to leave you."

Ella's breath caught in her throat, a strangled sound escaping her quivering lips. She stared at the man, mind unsteady with disbelief and desperation.

"Who, my brother?" she managed to choke out, clenching her fists at her sides.

The man only shrugged and looked off into the distance.

Ella's heart raced as she thought of her father, who had passed away ten years ago. In the wake of that loss, she remembered encounters with another homeless man who would greet her warmly, remarking on how she was growing into a fine young woman, always bringing her a sense of comfort. It felt as if her father was communicating through him.

Since then, she started to believe that many homeless people were no longer in control of all their senses and were often more like messengers of the spirit world, tuned into an otherworldly frequency ordinary people couldn't access.

Ella's heart pounded against her chest, a sickening fear settling in the pit of her stomach. The thought of him possibly talking about Oscar and offering a message from him from beyond the veil was all too much at that moment, paralyzing her with dread.

"Is he... dead?" Ella asked, her voice breaking at the last word.

The homeless man's eyes remained averted and vacant.

A sob escaped her as she reached out to steady herself against the building, the rough brick scraping her hand.

"Oh God, I have to go. I can't..."

She stumbled away, vision blurry with tears. The man's haunting words spun in dizzying circles around her mind.

If the man's words were a message from Oscar, that must mean he was truly dead. Maybe that is what Oscar was trying to tell her in her dream.

The thought was unbearable.

Oh Oscar, what has happened to you?

Chapter 2

The bell above the door chimed loudly as Ella entered Peggy's Coffeehouse. The rich, inviting aroma of freshly ground coffee beans and buttery pastries enveloped her, momentarily easing the tension that settled on her shoulders.

Behind the counter, Peg looked up from the coffee she was making, a warm smile spreading across her face at the sight of her stepdaughter. Her salt-and-pepper hair was pulled back into a loose ponytail, a few wispy strands framing her cherubic face.

Many locals affectionately called the shop "One-eyed Peg's," a playful nod to Peg's glass eye. With her characteristic resilience, Peg embraced the nickname wholeheartedly, often joking that it gave the place a unique character and charm.

"Ella, honey, I'm so glad you're here," Peg said, her voice as comforting as a hug. "I was beginning to worry about you."

In return, Ella managed to smile while hanging her coat on the hook by the door. "I'm sorry. I didn't mean to be late; I got sidetracked on the way here."

Peg's brow furrowed as she got a good look at Ella's face. "Is everything okay? You look like you've seen a ghost."

Ella's heart skipped a beat at the unintended accuracy of Peg's words. She swallowed hard and tried to compose herself, tying an apron around her waist. "I'm fine, really. Just a little tired. And everything going on with Oscar..."

She nodded, her expression soft with understanding. "I know it's been hard with Oscar gone. We all feel his absence."

"Thank you, Peg. I don't know what I'd do without you."

Peg smiled, her one good eye crinkling at the corner. "You'll never have to find out. I'm here for you, no matter what. We're family, after all."

She nodded, feeling warmth in her chest at the reminder. Peg had been more of a mother to her than her true mother had ever been. She entered Ella's life when she was around eleven, marrying her father and bringing a sense of stability to their household that she hadn't even realized was missing. Even after her father's passing, Peg remained a constant, supportive presence.

"I wish I could do more," Ella said, forcing a smile. "I feel so helpless just waiting for news."

Peg squeezed her hand, reminding her she was not alone in her pain. "We're all in this together, honey. And we'll get through it, one day at a time. Do you want to see if Todd needs any help in the back? I think I've got it covered out here for now."

Ella looked toward the kitchen, where she could hear the hiss of the industrial dishwasher. Todd, her stepbrother, had always been 'at home' working behind the scenes, preferring solitude rather than dealing with the constant stream of customers.

"Sure, I'll go check on him. Thanks."

As she made her way to the back of the shop, Ella couldn't shake the unease that settled into her consciousness.

She wondered if she should tell Peg about the encounter, about the cryptic message that had left her reeling. But something held her back, a fear that saying the words out loud would make them real in a way she wasn't ready to face.

The entire kitchen smelled of fresh banana bread. Todd stood at the sink, his back to her, scrubbing a pile of dishes with focused intensity. The clatter of dishes and the rush of running water nearly drowned out the sound of her footsteps as she approached.

"Hey, Todd," she said. "Peg said you could use some help back here."

Todd glanced over his shoulder, his dark eyes meeting hers momentarily before returning to his task. "Hey, Ella. I've got it. Everything's under control."

Ella frowned, sensing the tension in his voice. She knew that Oscar's disappearance had struck Todd hard. They were always close, bonded by their love of music.

"I know you can handle it," she said, stepping closer to the sink. "But that doesn't mean you have to do it alone."

Todd's shoulders slumped, a heavy sigh escaping his lips. He put down the plate he'd been scrubbing and rested his hands on the edge of the sink.

"I can't believe he's been gone this long. I keep expecting him to walk through that door and make some stupid joke about getting lost on the way to band practice or something."

Her heart dropped at the mention of the band, which Oscar and Todd started in high school. They'd spent countless hours practicing until their fingers bled and their voices grew hoarse.

Todd then turned to her, a heavy look on his face. "Do you think he might be dead? Or has he just gone missing?"

The question hung between them, shared grief a strange feeling to confront. Ella swallowed hard, her mind flashing back to the homeless man's cryptic message.

"I don't know," she admitted. "I get the sense that there's more to this than we know... like there's something we're missing."

Todd raised his brows, searching her eyes. "What do you mean? We've reached out to everyone we know."

Ella hesitated, torn between her desire to confide in her stepbrother and the fear of sounding crazy. But the look in Todd's eyes, the desperation, and hope, broke through her defenses.

"There's a homeless man I see sometimes on the way here." The words came out in a hurry. "He said something to me this morning..."

"Like what?"

"He said, 'he's sorry he had to leave.' I don't know; I think he was talking about Oscar."

Todd's mouth fell agape. "As if he knew something about what happened to him?"

Ella shook her head. "No, like he was carrying a message from Oscar. Like he was communicating through him."

"What? Why didn't you say anything?"

An awkward laugh escaped Ella's lips. "Because I don't want to sound crazy. Because I wasn't sure if it was real or if I was imagining things."

He reached across the counter to take her hand. His skin was rough against hers, and she could feel the calluses on his fingers from years of playing guitar.

"I don't know what to do," Ella continued, hardly comforted. "I feel like I'm losing my mind, seeing and hearing things that can't be real. But I can't ignore it either."

"You're not crazy, Ella. If there's even a chance that this man knows something about Oscar, we've got to look into it."

Ella nodded; her throat was too tight to speak. She held onto Todd's hand, trying hard to draw strength from his touch.

"I miss him so much," she said. "I feel like a part of me is missing, and I'll never be whole again."

His eyes grew weary, and he gently stroked her hand, fingertips tracing her skin with tenderness. "I know. I feel the same way. But we'll find him, Ella. We'll bring him home, whatever it takes."

As the morning rush began to subside, Ella found a moment to catch her breath. She closed her eyes briefly, breathing in the sweet scent of cinnamon rolls baking in the oven.

When she opened them again, she saw Todd coming out of the kitchen, wiping his hands on his apron. His dark hair looked like it hadn't been washed in days, and dark circles rested heavily beneath his eyes.

Her heart clenched at the sight of him, remembering the revelation he had shared with her just a few months ago. She always knew that Todd and Oscar were close. Still, she never suspected the depth of their connection until Todd had broken down and confessed everything.

It was a shock. She and everyone else had always assumed Todd's affection for Oscar was platonic, a brotherly bond forged through shared experiences and family history. But as he poured his heart out, voice weak with emotion, she realized how much he truly loved Oscar.

"I didn't mean for it to happen," Todd had said. "We were just close at first, you know? But then one night, we were up late writing songs together, and something just... clicked. It was like we saw each other for the first time, really saw each other."

Ella remembers listening in stunned silence, her mind reeling with the implications of his confession. She had always known that Oscar was gay. Still, the idea of him being in a relationship with their stepbrother... was almost too much to comprehend.

But when she looked at Todd now, saw the pain and sorrow etched into every line of his face, she couldn't find it in herself to judge him. He was suffering as much as she was, maybe even more, considering the depth of his feelings for Oscar.

She always suspected there was more to their relationship than met the eye, but she never imagined this.

Ella thought back over the past year, trying to pinpoint the moments when things had changed between Oscar and Todd. Had there been signs she missed? Lingering glances, secret smiles, hushed conversations that stopped when she entered the room? In the end, it made sense.

A pang of guilt entered her lungs. How could she have been so blind? Oscar was her twin, her other half. They shared everything. At least, she thought so...

She remembered the day Oscar had come out to her, his voice shaking with nerves as he told her he was gay. They were so young then. She hugged him tightly and told him that she loved him no matter what. But even then, he didn't mention Todd.

All those times she confided in Todd about her worries for Oscar and how he had always been there to listen and offer comfort made her wonder. As she watched Todd work, his movements smooth and practiced, she began to sense something was being hidden.

What else had Oscar confided in Todd that might be a secret?

Adelaide stood in front of the mirror, applying the final touches of her lipstick. She smoothed her hair, making sure every strand was in place. The room behind her was immaculate. Not a single item was out of order.

She watched the clock on the wall, heart fluttering with anticipation. Frank would be here any minute. Adelaide had been looking forward to this moment all week, a chance to steal some precious time with him while Ella was at work.

As if on cue, there was a knock at the door. She took a deep breath, smoothing her blouse one last time before opening it.

Frank stood there, relaxed, his toolbox in hand and a smile on his rugged face. "Morning, Adelaide." His voice was deep and warm.

Adelaide felt a shiver run through her at the sound of it. "Good morning, Frank," she said, stepping aside to let him in. "So glad you could make it here."

Frank set down his toolbox, his eyes glancing appreciatively over her form. "Wouldn't miss it for the world," he said, pulling her into his arms. "You know I always make time for your... maintenance requests."

Adelaide melted into his embrace, taking in the scent of his aftershave. For a moment, all her worries and fears melted away, lost in the sensation of his muscular arms around her.

But Adelaide felt something was wrong even while surrendering to his touch. The flickering lights in the apartment and the strange noises in the walls all seemed to point to something sinister, something she couldn't quite put her finger on.

She stepped back and looked up at Frank with troubled eyes. "Frank, have you noticed anything strange in the building lately?"

Frank frowned. "Strange how?"

Adelaide hesitated, her brow furrowing as she struggled to articulate her concerns. "Just... strange things," she began. "Lights flickering, weird sounds. Sometimes, it's like the entire building is alive."

She paused, standing stiffly while searching Frank's face for any sign of understanding. He just stared back.

"Oh, it's probably nothing," she added hastily, gesturing her hand. But even as the words left her mouth, she couldn't shake the nagging feeling that something was wrong. The eerie sensations that plagued her for days refused to be ignored.

Frank's face softened, and he pulled her closer soothingly. "Hey, don't worry about it. I'm sure it's just old wiring or something. I'll have a look at it later, okay?"

Adelaide nodded, trying to push her fears aside. She knew she was being paranoid, but with Oscar's disappearance weighing heavily on her mind, it was hard not to make even the most mundane occurrences seem odd. Everything in her life was different.

Despite Frank's reassuring presence, she still somehow believed the building held secrets. Or, perhaps her son's disappearance was all too much to handle. For now, she tried to focus on the moment, reeling from the promise of a few stolen hours together.

The rest of the world could wait.

Chapter 3

Ella trudged up the beat-up stairs of the apartment building, bypassing the elevator. Her steps were sluggish from the day's events, the smell of stale cigarette smoke assaulting her nostrils.

She made her way down the dim hallway and paused at the door to her apartment, keeping a hand hovered over the brass knob. The muffled sound of the television seeped through the thin walls, and she could almost picture her mother sprawled on the couch, a half-empty bottle of wine dangling from her fingertips.

With a sigh, Ella pushed open the door and stepped inside, the familiar scent of her childhood home washing over her—including the light floral perfume her mother favored, a blend of jasmine and rose that felt equal parts comforting and suffocating.

The living room was shrouded in darkness, and the only light source was the glow of the television.

"Mom?" Ella called out, voice tinged with concern.

Adelaide's head lifted from the couch. Her eyes were wide and unfocused, bloodshot from the wine and hours of staring at the television. "Ella? Is that you?" she slurred, squinting into the dimness.

Ella dropped her keys on the cluttered kitchen table, the sharp sound echoing in the small apartment.

"Yes. I'm back from work." Her tone was flat and resigned as she shrugged off her coat and draped it over a nearby chair.

Adelaide sat up straight, her movements unsteady as she gripped the arm of the couch for support. "How'd it go? Was Todd there?" Her fingers tightened around the neck of the wine bottle.

Ella's stomach clenched at the mention of her stepbrother, their earlier conversation still fresh in her mind. She shook her head, not wanting to go into it.

"It was fine," she finally replied, hesitation clear. "But there's something I want to tell you. Something that happened on the way to work this morning. It's... well, it's a bit strange."

Adelaide's brow furrowed, and she leaned forward. "What is it?"

Ella sat on the edge of the couch, her hands clasped tightly in her lap. She took a deep breath, readying herself for what was to come.

"I saw that homeless man today," she began, her voice barely above a whisper. "You know, the one usually hanging around the neighborhood with those haunting light blue eyes. The one we've seen a few times near the subway station." Ella paused, swallowing hard. "He said something to me that I think was meant to be about Oscar. It was... unsettling."

Adelaide's eyes widened, her face starting to drain of color. The wine bottle trembled slightly in her grasp. "What did he say?"

She met her mother's gaze, her own eyes reflecting a mix of confusion and hope. "His exact words were, 'he's sorry he had to leave.' It was like he knew something about what happened to Oscar."

"Oh, my God," she breathed, her voice trembling. "What do you think it means? Could it really be about Oscar?"

"I don't know, Mom..." She tried to calm her wavering voice, her chin beginning to quiver. She wrapped her arms around herself tightly as if seeking comfort. "It felt like he was trying to tell me something important, but I couldn't understand what exactly."

Her mother's eyes darted around the room, pausing briefly on the shadows cast onto the floor from the harsh television lighting. "I've sensed something, Ella," she said, her voice barely above a whisper. "Something strange, like Oscar... might be trying to reach out to us. From wherever he is."

A shiver ran down Ella's back, goosebumps rising on her arms. "What do you mean?

Adelaide leaned forward, and her voice dropped to a conspiratorial whisper. "The lights, Ella. Haven't you noticed how they've been flickering lately? If he is... if he's dead," she swallowed, her eyes gleaming with fear as if the sentence alone was too much to handle, "maybe he's trying to send us a message? Maybe this is his way of letting us know?"

Ella's thoughts flashed back to the eerie shadows in the hallway, the way the fluorescent lights had sputtered and died as she walked by. She had chalked it up to faulty wiring that some mice had chewed on. But now, she wasn't so sure.

"I don't know, Mom. It could just be a coincidence." She wanted to believe it, but facing such strange occurrences would only add to the confusion of grief—plus, the rational part of her mind was beginning to resist the idea upon hearing it from her drunken mother.

Adelaide shook her head vehemently, eyes blazing with conviction. "No. It's him. I feel it in my bones. Something has happened, something terrible, and he's trying to tell us."

Ella hesitated, torn between comforting her mother and facing the harsh reality. "No," she said finally, her voice now firm. "We must keep looking for answers to find out what happened to him. We can't just assume..."

Adelaide nodded, tears now running freely down her cheeks. "I just miss him so much. I don't know how to keep going without him. Every day feels like an eternity."

Ella frowned at the raw pain in her mother's weak voice. She pulled her into a tight hug, feeling the shudder of her sobs against her chest—the familiar scent of her mother's perfume stronger aside the salty tang of tears. Seeing her mother so vulnerable tore her heart into pieces.

"Shh, Mom. It's okay. It's all going to be okay."

Adelaide clung to her, barely whispering. Her tone was full of shudders and breathless hiccups, making it nearly impossible to make out her words. "I can't lose him, Ella. I can't. I promised I would always keep you both safe. Now he's gone, and I don't know what to do."

A sharp knock on the door shook them from the embrace. Ella's heart raced as she stood up and pulled away from her mother.

"Christ, I forgot that detective said she'd be stopping by today," Adelaide remembered, her voice hoarse from crying.

Ella crossed the room on shaky legs, a hand trembling as she reached out for the doorknob.

With a deep breath, she turned the knob and pulled the door open, revealing a slender woman with wise brown eyes and a no-nonsense expression. She wore a tailored suit and held a gold badge that glittered in the dim, yellow hallway lights.

"Good evening. I'm Detective Dingess." Her voice carried a professional blend of empathy and intelligence. "I hope I'm not interrupting anything."

"No, not at all," she replied, casually patting her eyes with her sleeve. "Please, come in."

Detective Dingess entered the apartment, her eyes scanning the room with the practiced gaze of a seasoned investigator. She nodded in greeting to Adelaide before turning her attention back to Ella.

"Thank you for seeing me tonight. I will be taking over the lead on Oscar's disappearance. I realize these visits can be difficult, so please call me Dory. It's short for Dorianne." She punctuated her name with a small, reassuring smile.

Ella led the detective to the kitchen table and gestured for her to sit. Adelaide hovered nervously nearby, the wine bottle now set aside on the floor.

Detective Dingess surveyed the apartment, gaze lingering on the surging lights. "Electrical problems?"

"The building's falling apart," muttered Adelaide from the corner.

The detective nodded and pulled out a notepad. "I've already familiarized myself with Oscar's case, but I want to review everything from the beginning. With that being said, when did you last see your brother, Ella?"

Ella swallowed hard, the question already making her head swim. "It's been eight days now. I went to see him at Peggy's Coffeehouse."

"And you, Mrs. Young?" Dingess turned to Adelaide.

Adelaide looked up, her voice small. "The same: eight days ago. He kissed me goodbye and said he'd see me for dinner. He never showed up."

The detective scribbled some quick notes on the paper, the pen loud in the quiet room. "Any idea where he might have gone? Friends he might stay with?"

Ella shook her head. "No, he would have told us. I can't imagine why he would disappear like this. It's not like him."

"Sometimes people keep secrets, even from those closest to them." The detective's words hung heavy in the air, laden with implication. "I need to look at his room. Is that okay with you all?"

Adelaide nodded wearily and pointed down the dark hallway. "It's the one at the end. Ella's been there since..." She trailed off purposefully, the rest of the sentence stowed away, creating an ache in her chest.

Dory nodded sympathetically, eyes softened. She went down the narrow corridor to Oscar's room, taking in the peeling paint and water-stained ceiling. The building's state of disrepair was apparent.

Inside the room, her gaze settled on a framed photograph perched precariously on the cluttered dresser. She picked it up, studying the image of Ella and Oscar, their arms wrapped tightly around each other, both grinning widely at the camera.

"Ella, do you mind if I ask you a few more questions?" Detective Dingess called out, her voice echoing slightly in the room.

Ella appeared in the doorway, her slim frame seeming to shrink as she hugged herself tightly. It was as if she was physically holding herself together. "Of course."

The detective carefully placed the photo back on the dresser, her fingers lingering momentarily on the frame. "Is there anything else you can think of that might help us find Oscar? Any detail, no matter how small or insignificant. It could be crucial."

Ella hesitated. She thought of the homeless man's words. Normally, she wouldn't give the homeless man the time of day, but now she was placing the weight of the world onto what he said to her.

"There's something else," she began quietly. "It's probably nothing, but... I had a strange encounter this morning on my way to work."

Detective Dingess leaned forward, her interest piqued. "Go on," she encouraged, pen gripped and prepared to write on the notepad.

Ella fidgeted with the hem of her shirt, avoiding the detective's piercing gaze. "There's this homeless man I often see on my way to work. Today, he said something... odd."

The detective's eyebrows raised fractionally, just enough to tell that she was listening. "What did he say?"

"He said, 'he's sorry he had to leave.' I know it sounds crazy, but I couldn't help feeling like he was talking about Oscar."

Detective Dingess remained silent for a moment, her expression unreadable. Ella felt her cheeks flush with embarrassment.

"I feel silly even mentioning it," she added quickly, shaking her head. "It's probably nothing. Just a coincidence, or my mind playing tricks on me."

The detective finally nodded, jotting something down in the notepad. "Don't dismiss your instincts, Ella. Sometimes, the smallest details can be important. Can you describe this homeless man?"

She closed her eyes, trying to recall the man's features. "He has long, tangled hair and a scraggly beard. His clothes are dirty and worn. But his eyes... they're a startling blue. Clear and sharp, despite everything else about him looking so rough. For lack of a better word."

Detective Dingess wrote down the description, pen scratching against the paper. "And where exactly did you see him?"

"On the corner of 86th and 4th, near the subway station," Ella replied, her voice growing stronger as she focused on the details. "He's there most mornings."

"Thank you. I know it wasn't easy to share that." The acknowledgment of her anxiety was small, but it calmed Ella a bit. "We'll look into it, along with everything else. Can you recall anything else about the last time you saw your brother?"

Ella's mouth was suddenly dry. "The day before he went missing, we had dinner together. He seemed fine. Happy, even. He was excited about a new song he was working on with Todd—Todd is our stepbrother."

The detective nodded and jotted down some notes as they paced to the kitchen. "And did he mention anything out of the ordinary? Any plans or appointments that were unusual or unexpected?" she pressed, eyes scanning Ella's face for any hint of recollection.

Ella shook her head, frowning as she tried to remember. She absentmindedly tucked a strand of hair behind her ear. "No, nothing like that. He was just Oscar. My goofy, talented, wonderful brother." Her voice caught slightly on the last few words, fondness coloring her tone.

Detective Dingess shifted to Adelaide. "And what about you, Ms. Young? Did you notice anything strange or out of place in the days leading up to Oscar's disappearance?"

Adelaide's face crumpled, eyes filling with raw tears that threatened to spill over at any moment. Her hands trembled, and she clasped them tightly in her lap, willing them to stop. "No, nothing. He was my sweet, precious boy. I can't believe he's gone."

"We will do everything in our power to find out what happened to your son and brother. I promise you that." She reached out and placed a reassuring hand on Adelaide's shoulder.

As the questioning continued, Adelaide sat beside Ella. She had stopped crying, but her face was left puffy and red, her eyes glazed with a dull, hollow look.

"Ella," Detective Dingess said determinedly, turning her head. "I understand you and your brother were very close. Twins, right? Can you tell me a little more about your relationship?"

"Sure. We were like best friends. We've done... We did everything together since we were little. He's the one person I could always count on, no matter what." Ella's voice wavered as she explained, recalling the countless memories she shared with him.

She felt the tears well up in her eyes, but she blinked them back, determined to maintain her composure. She couldn't break down now, not in front of the detective. She wanted to stay strong, for Oscar's sake and for the sake of finding him. This information was crucial. Her fingers twisted in her lap, a nervous habit she developed since her brother's disappearance.

Detective Dingess probed with more questions, her gaze shifting between the two of them, keen eyes taking in every nuance of their expressions and body language. "Is there anything else you can tell me about Oscar? Any recent changes in his behavior or lifestyle?"

Adelaide's eyes darted to her daughter as if seeking confirmation. The tension in her shoulders was visible. "He's always been a bit of a free spirit, but lately, he seemed more distant. Like he had something on his mind." Her tone grew quiet, unspoken worries hanging in the air.

"And what about his relationship with the two of you?" Detective Dingess asked, ready to capture any crucial information onto her notepad. The question hung in the air, heavy with implications.

After a moment, Adelaide pressed her lips into a thin line. "We had our troubles, like any family. But we loved each other. We always will," she stated firmly as if she was daring Dingess to question the depth of their familial bond further.

Ella reached over and squeezed her mother's hand, a silent show of support, hoping to relax the budding feelings from her mother. The gesture spoke volumes about their complicated relationship, united in this crisis despite their past differences. The room fell silent for a moment, filled only with the weight of unspoken words and the shared pain of grief.

"And what about your living situation?" Detective Dingess asked after a beat of silence, gaze hovering sharply over the two. "I understand you recently moved back in with your mother. Is that correct?"

"Yes," Ella said, looking at Adelaide. "I was meant to move to London with my boyfriend last week but couldn't leave after Oscar disappeared. Nothing felt right. I had nowhere else to stay, having already moved out of my apartment. Now I'm staying here until I find out what happened to him." Ella's chin quivered. "I'm not...'

Just then, there was a loud screeching sound as Iris began hissing loudly at something outside the window.

"Quiet, you mangy creature," Adelaide barked, her gaze fixed on Iris as she stood up on the windowsill, back arched. "That damned cat. I don't know why Ella always wanted one. Guess she still does."

Adelaide pushed her chair back from the kitchen table, practically knocking it over, and walked to the window. She peered out, scanning the street below for whatever caught Iris's attention.

Detective Dingess' ears perked up, but she thought it best to ignore Adelaide's behavior. The seasoned investigator had learned long ago that silence was sometimes the most effective tool in her arsenal.

Turning back to Ella, the detective leaned in slightly, her voice low and measured. "Alright, don't shoot the messenger here, but your mother has quite the reputation in this building." She was careful with her words. "There are rumors of her drinking all hours and having an affair with the maintenance man, Frank. Are these things true?"

Her piercing gaze never wavered from Ella's face, searching for any hint of deception. But Ella was truthful, nodding hesitantly, eyes darting briefly to her mother's back—she still looked out of the window. "I've heard those rumors too."

Ella glanced nervously at Adelaide, voice barely above a whisper. "But my mom has had a difficult time since Oscar disappeared."

Adelaide returned to the kitchen table, and they both quickly and silently gauged her reaction.

Dory searched Ella's expression with narrowed eyes. "For someone so close to their sibling, I have the feeling you might know more than you *think* you know about your brother's disappearance."

Adelaide exploded in anger as she settled into her chair, face contorted with rage. "She always hated Oscar!" Spittle flew from her lips. "She even wished he was dead!" Her accusation echoed off the walls of the small apartment, making them both flinch.

Heat rose in Ella's cheeks as she vehemently denied the accusation. "What are you talking about? That's not true!" She cried, voice cracking with emotion. Her hands clenched into fists at her sides, trembling with despair. "I love Oscar. He means everything to me. You're just a mean old drunk who drove him away!"

Detective Dingess paused, gesturing with her hands for the both of them to calm down. The emotional strain in the room was palpable, and she knew she needed to regain control of the situation before tensions grew stronger. After gathering her thoughts again, she resumed the questioning, calm and insistent. "Is there anything else you can tell me about Oscar before I go? Have there been any *other* recent changes in his behavior or lifestyle?"

"You should talk to Peg, my ex-husband's wife," Adelaide said quickly, her voice laced with bitterness as she crossed her arms. "She's always been too lenient with the boys, letting them run wild without consequences."

Dory raised her eyebrows. "What do you mean, exactly?" she pressed on, sensing there was more to this statement than what met the eye.

Adelaide leaned forward, her eyes darting around the room as if checking for eavesdroppers. "Oscar and Todd, they were involved. Romantically. It's sick, it's wrong. And Peg just let it happen under her roof like it was the most normal thing in the world."

Ella shifted in her seat, barely able to process the words coming from her mother's mouth.

Dory's pen halted mid-sentence, hovering above the notepad. Her eyes widened in surprise, and she momentarily struggled to maintain a professional composure. "Oscar and Todd were involved?" she repeated.

Adelaide nodded vigorously. "I couldn't believe it when I found out. My son with his stepbrother. It's unnatural."

Ella felt her stomach clench painfully, a wave of nausea rising in her throat like bile. She'd been dreading this moment, hoping that the detective wouldn't ask about the complicated, tangled web of their family dynamics. The secrets they'd all been keeping threatened to spill out, and she wasn't sure she was ready for the consequences.

But as she sat there trembling, Ella knew she couldn't lie. She couldn't hide the truth anymore, not if she wanted to find out what had happened to her brother. Whatever the cost, she had to speak up and tell Detective Dingess everything she knew.

"They are very close," Ella interjected, trying to ease the conversation. "Closer than most stepbrothers, but I guess that's because they had a lot in common, with their music and their… their struggles with identity," she stammered.

"How serious was their relationship?"

Adelaide shrugged, taking the question as her own. Her shoulders hunched as she spoke. "Serious enough. They were always sneaking around, whispering to each other. I caught them kissing in the kitchen once. I almost threw up."

Dory leaned back in her chair, absorbing this new information. "And you think Peg is to blame for their relationship?"

Adelaide nodded, her eyes blazing. "She's always been too soft on them. Let them do whatever they want, with no consequences. If she had stopped it, maybe none of this would have happened."

Detective Dingess' pen scratched furiously across the page. "So, it sounds like it was a serious relationship. Did they ever talk about running away together or making plans for the future?"

Ella could feel her mother stiffen, waves of anger rolling off her.

"Who knows? It was sick," Adelaide spat, her voice shaking with barely suppressed rage. "Disgusting. Her own son, seducing his stepbrother... it's just so wrong."

Dory tapped her pen against her notepad and closed it, her brow furrowed. "I need to talk to Peg and Todd and get their side of the story."

Adelaide scoffed. "Good luck getting anything out of them. They're probably too busy trying to cover for each other."

As soon as Dory left, Adelaide's cheeks flushed with anger as she turned to Ella. "Why did you blab about Frank? You had no right to say anything!"

Ella explained that it was only a rumor and that the detective had brought it up first, but her mother had cut her off mid-sentence. "Frank is a good man who has always been there for us, and I won't let his reputation be tarnished because of your loose tongue! Now get out of my sight!"

Feeling guilty and embarrassed, Ella retreated to her bedroom, her mother's words still ringing in her ears. She closed the door behind her with a soft click, leaning against it momentarily as she tried to gather her thoughts.

Lying on the bed, Ella replayed the conversation with the detective in her mind. She had hoped it would bring some answers about Oscar's disappearance, but it only brought more confusion.

She rolled onto her side, hugging a pillow close to her body as if it could shield her from the turmoil swirling around her. Sensing her distress, Iris jumped onto the bed and curled up next to her, the warmth of the cat lulling Ella to sleep.

She awoke, her blurred eyes slowly emerging from an unintended slumber. The ambiance was abruptly shattered by shrill cries reverberating from her mother's bedroom down the hall.

Faster than ever, she made her way towards her mother's door. Adelaide's voice grew louder and more frantic as she approached, making Ella's heart thump like a drum in her chest.

The lamp by her mother's bed flickered ominously, casting eerie shadows that danced across the walls. Adelaide's screams became more coherent, directed at an unseen entity that only she could perceive.

"Stop it!" Adelaide cried, tears streaming down her face, leaving glistening trails on her cheeks. Her voice cracked with emotion as she pleaded, "Oscar... why are you doing this to me?"

Ella realized her mother thought she was talking to Oscar's ghost. She couldn't move or speak, frozen in fear as her mother turned to look at her with a sad expression on her face.

"I can't take it anymore, Ella. I can't continue to live like this!" Adelaide yanked the lamp's cord from the wall, plunging the room into blackness.

Chapter 4

Detective Dingess paused at the first door on her list, a battered wooden frame with peeling green paint. The brass number 2B hung crooked as if it was clinging to its last threads of dignity, and long shadows cast across the hallway, seeming to dance on the carpet with every step she took.

Dingess raised her hand softly and knocked on the door, the sound echoing through the empty corridor like a gunshot. She could hear muffled movement from inside, the scraping of furniture against the floor, and a short turn of the knob.

The door creaked open, revealing a small, wrinkled face peering out from the shadows. The woman's eyes were a watery blue, her skin lined and weathered like a piece of old parchment. Her thin, silver hair was pulled back into a tight bun, furthering her look of stern fragility.

"Yes?" the woman asked, voice thin and reedy. "Can I help you?" Her gnarled fingers gripped the door as if she was ready to slam it shut at a moment's notice.

Dory flashed her badge, the gold gleaming in the dim light of the hallway. "Detective Dorianne Dingess, NYPD. I'm investigating the disappearance of Oscar Young. I was hoping you could answer some questions."

She kept her tone professional yet gentle, knowing that cooperation often depended on first impressions, especially with elderly witnesses who might be easily startled or confused.

The woman's eyes widened in surprise, a flicker of recognition passing across her weathered features. "Oscar? The young man from 7C? Oh, how terrible! Please, come in." Her demeanor immediately softened, concern etching deeper lines into her already well-mapped face. The initial wariness melted away, replaced by genuine worry for her neighbor.

She stepped back, her slippers shuffling against the worn rug. She made a wide gesture to the inside of the apartment, allowing Dingess to enter.

Inside, it was slightly musty-smelling and cramped. The living room was a jumble of mismatched furniture and piles of old newspapers. The air hung thick with the scent of mothballs and a layer of dust. Faded photographs filled the walls, telling the story of long life and memories, faces from different eras smiling inside the ornate frames. Knick-knacks and mementos crowded nearly every available surface.

Dingess sat on the edge of a green armchair, a notebook on her knee. It creaked under her weight but held firm. "Thank you for your time, Mrs...?" She left the question hanging, pen stable against the paper, ready to scratch down the woman's name.

"Lebowitz," the woman said, settling on the couch with a slight grunt. "Esther Lebowitz. I've lived in this building for forty years, Detective. Seen many people come and go." Her eyes looked distant, like she was mentally flipping through decades of memories.

Dingess leaned forward with her elbows on her knees. "What can you tell me about the Young family, Mrs. Lebowitz? Did you know them well?" She kept her voice calm, encouraging the older woman to feel at ease.

Esther's face creased into a frown, and she fiddled with a loose thread on the outside of her sweater. "Not well, no. They kept to themselves, mostly. But I remember when they first moved in. They were very young then."

"And what about the children?" Dingess asked carefully. She lifted her pen as she spoke, leaving her hands in a relaxed position. "Oscar and his sister, Ella. Did you ever see them much while they were growing up?"

"Those poor children," she sighed. "They had it rough growing up in that household. With their mother's drinking and their father's... well, his absence."

Within a beat of silence, her forehead furrowed in concentration. She tacked on her words carefully. "There was another boy, I think... maybe younger than Oscar and Ella. I haven't seen him in years, though. Come to think of it, I can't even remember his name." Her voice trailed off, uncertainty clouding her eyes, and she shifted her gaze to the window slowly. "I always wondered what happened to him."

The detective's heart skipped. "Another boy?" She tried to keep the surprise out of her voice, not wanting to influence Esther's memory.

"Of course, I could be confusing things. After all, it was quite a while ago," Esther said slowly as if she were straining to recall the details. "But I do remember him being very handsome. He had a smile that could light up a room, that much I'm certain of."

"And what about Adelaide?" She carefully steered the conversation. "What can you tell me about her?"

Esther's face twisted into a grimace, and she locked eyes with the detective as if her memory had been triggered. "That woman... she's trouble, Detective. Always has been. Drinking, yelling, all hours of the night. And the way she treated those kids..." Her voice dropped to a whisper despite her agitation, heavy with unspoken accusations.

She shook her head, silver hair catching the light. Her words flew out now as if a dam had broken. "I've heard things. Things that make my blood run cold. The way she yells at them... it's not right. No child should have to endure that kind of treatment." Esther's hands trembled slightly as she spoke, her distress palpable. The room seemed to grow colder as the weight of her words settled.

Dory's stomach clenched, a cold fury burning in her veins. She had seen too many cases like this, too many children suffering at the hands of those who were supposed to protect them. But to preserve her professionalism, she straightened her tone.

"Mrs. Lebowitz, is there anything else you can think of that might be important about Oscar's disappearance? Any unusual occurrences or strange visitors in the days leading up to it?"

Esther considered the question, fingers tapping a restless rhythm on the wooden arm of the chair. "Well, now that you mention it, there was an argument just a few days before he went missing."

"Go on," she encouraged gently.

"It was late, around midnight. I was awake because my arthritis was acting up. I heard voices in the hallway, angry ones." She shook her head, a troubled expression crossing her features. "It was Oscar and that stepbrother of his... Todd, I think. They were bickering about something, but I couldn't make out what."

Dingess' eyebrows raised slightly. "Did you hear anything specific?"

Esther's lips pressed into a thin line. "Not really, but it sounded serious. Then I heard a door slam, and everything went quiet." Her shoulders sagged. "I should have said something sooner, but... well, you know how it is. You don't want to get involved in other people's business."

Dingess nodded sympathetically, scribbling furiously in her notebook. This new information could be crucial to the investigation. "Any other details that stood out to you, Mrs. Lebowitz?"

Her eyes clouded over as she searched her memory. After a moment, she shook her head.

"I'm sorry, Detective. I wish I could be of more help, but that's all I can remember. My mind isn't what it used to be..."

Dory closed her notebook and tucked it back into her jacket pocket. She met Esther's gaze warmly, voice laced with gratitude. "Mrs. Lebowitz, you've been incredibly helpful regardless. Thank you for taking the time to speak with me today."

The detective stood up, the old armchair creaking in relief. Esther struggled to her feet in succession, joints protesting the movement. "I hope you find that poor young man. He was so kind—he always helped me with my groceries when he saw me struggling."

Dingess offered a soft smile. "We're doing everything we can, Mrs. Lebowitz. Every piece of information helps, and what you've told me today could be very important to our investigation."

As they made their way to the door, Esther's gnarled hand reached out to touch Dingess' arm. She flinched slightly at the contact but turned to meet the woman's eyes.

"Detective, do be careful. There's something not right about that family."

Dingess nodded, her expression serious. Her stomach twisted slightly at the implications. "I understand, Mrs. Lebowitz. Thank you again for your time."

With a nod of appreciation, she stepped out into the dimly lit hallway, leaving Esther in the doorway with a worried expression.

Dingess couldn't shake the feeling she was missing something. Some vital clue, some hidden connection, would tie all the disparate threads together. At least, that's what she hoped. The mention of another boy nagged at her mind, a loose end that demanded her attention.

She shook her head and moved on to the next door, deciding that answers would not come by ruminating. She tapped her knuckles against the worn wood, and after a moment, the door pulled open. A middle-aged woman answered—her disheveled appearance and weary face suggested that the unexpected visitor caught her off guard.

"Detective Dingess, NYPD." Her voice was firm but not unkind as she flashed her badge. "I'm investigating the disappearance of Oscar Young. Do you mind if I ask you a few questions?"

She keenly studied the woman's face, searching for any flicker of recognition or unease at the mention of Oscar's name.

The woman hesitated, eyes darting nervously down the hallway before settling back on Dingess. She looked clearly uncomfortable with the situation. After a moment's deliberation, she conceded. "I suppose. But I don't know much. We keep to ourselves here."

The notion hung heavy in the air—this was not where people asked questions or got involved in each other's business.

"Any information could be helpful, no matter how small," Dingess reassured. "Did you know the family well?"

"Not really," the woman answered, leaning against the doorframe. "Adelaide kept to herself mostly, always has. But I remember her kids, Oscar, and his twin sister. Thick as thieves, those two. Always laughing, always together. It was sweet, you know?"

Dingess scribbled a note in her notebook. "Was there anyone else living with them? Another boy, maybe?"

The woman searched her memory. "Come to think of it, yes. There was another boy, Todd. I think his name was. He was a quiet guy who kept to himself, but I haven't seen him in years. Funny how you forget things like that."

"Right, Todd, his stepbrother."

The neighbor leaned in, her wrinkled face creasing further as she lowered her voice. The smell of lavender perfume wafted between them. "Well, it's no secret she's a drunk. Adelaide, I mean. She was always yelling, making a racket at all hours. God knows how often I've been woken up by her carrying on. And rumor has it she's been getting cozy with Frank, our maintenance man. Not that it's any of my business, but you see things when you've lived here as long as I have."

"I heard something about that. Perhaps it's time I talked with Frank." Dingess tapped her pen thoughtfully against the page. "You've been very helpful. I appreciate you taking the time to speak with me."

"Of course, Detective. But please don't mention what I said about Frank. We all have to live here, you know? I don't want any trouble."

"No worries," Dingess assured her with a firm nod. "Everything you've told me is confidential. I hope you have a nice day."

She turned and walked down the dimly lit hall. The faded carpet muffled her steps as she walked.

The detective spotted Frank emerging from a supply closet, his graying hair disheveled. He wiped a smudge of dirt from his cheek. She approached him with purposeful strides. "Detective Dingess. Do you have a minute?"

Frank paused, a wrench still in his grip. "Yes, Detective. What can I do for you?"

"I wanted to get your thoughts on what might have happened to Oscar."

Unease crossed his weathered face as he said, "I don't know much about Oscar's disappearance. It's all been a shock to everyone here. Oscar was always friendly, always had a smile for everyone," he added, his gruff voice carrying a hint of nostalgia. "I can't imagine what might've happened to him."

Dingess studied him intently, intuition tingling. She noticed the slight tension in his shoulders and how his eyes darted briefly to the side. "You're close to Adelaide, aren't you? I hear the two of you spend a lot of time together," she probed gently, keeping her voice neutral and her gaze sharp.

Frank's jaw tightened almost imperceptibly, and he took a deep breath before answering. "Yes, we're friendly. She's going through a tough time with her son missing. I try to be there for her when I can, you know?"

"I understand, Frank. If there's anything you can think of, no matter how small it may seem, it could make a significant difference in this case."

"Look, those kids... they've been through enough. Oscar and Ella, they're good kids. I want to help in any way I can. But I don't know what else to tell you." His voice carried a hint of frustration.

"Well, if you think of anything, call me." She handed him her card with a nod.

Dory stepped inside and took in the atmosphere of Peg's coffeehouse. Mismatched chairs and overstuffed couches were scattered throughout the room, the walls covered with bookshelves and local artwork. The murmur of conversation and the clatter of ceramic cups filled the air, a soothing backdrop to the shop's daily atmosphere. Peg looked up from behind the counter, her one good eye narrowing as she recognized the detective.

Dingess nodded and made her way over. "Peg Young? I spoke to you on the phone earlier."

Peg wiped her hands on her apron, a sad smile playing at the corners of her mouth. "Of course. Please, have a seat. I'll be right with you."

She turned to the young man working next to her, his dark hair falling into his eyes as he focused on the latte he was making. "Todd, can you take over for a while? I need to talk to the detective."

Todd looked up. "Sure, Mom. No problem."

Peg led Dingess to a small table in the corner, far away from the louder areas of the coffeehouse. They both settled down comfortably.

"I can only imagine how difficult this must be for you," Dingess began softly, heart aching for the woman before her.

Peg nodded, her eyes glistening with unshed tears. "Thank you, Detective. It's been a nightmare this past week, not knowing where Oscar is or what has happened to him."

"I understand, Mrs. Young. And I promise I'm doing everything possible to find the truth—but I do need your help."

Peg took a deep breath. "Of course. Anything you need, just ask."

Dingess leaned forward. "Can you tell me about your relationship with Adelaide? I understand there was some," she thought of a light term to describe their dynamic. "tension between the two of you."

Peg's face tightened. "Well, Adelaide and I... we have a complicated history. I was young and foolish when I met her then-husband, Mitch. He didn't tell me he was married until much later after I fell in love with him. By then, it was too late, and I came to believe that he was the answer to all my problems. I never meant to hurt Adelaide or the children." The weight of her past decisions was evident in her voice.

"Please tell me more about that. Any conflicts or tensions that might be relevant?"

"Where do I even start?" Peg sighed. "Adelaide never forgave me for the affair, and she made damn sure the kids knew about it, too. Oscar and Ella were caught in the middle, torn between their parents."

Detective Dingess wrote a few quick words in the notebook. "And your relationship with Adelaide now is...?"

"Strained." The words rushed out. "We tolerate each other for the children's sake, but no love is lost between us. She blames me for breaking up her marriage, and I don't think she'll ever let go of that."

"And what about Oscar and Todd? Were you aware of their close relationship?"

Her face crumpled, a single tear slipping down her cheek. "I... I suspected, I suppose, long before I knew. The way they looked at each other always seemed to be together, and it was hard not to see it. I should've said something or done something. But I couldn't bear to see them torn apart. They were happy together, so in love..."

Just then, Todd emerged from the back room carrying a tray of freshly baked pastries. He stopped in his tracks when he saw them.

The detective turned to him. "Todd. I was hoping to ask you some questions as well."

Todd put down the tray, his hands shaking slightly. "Of course. Anything I can do to help."

Peg gave him a warning look, but Todd ignored it, focusing entirely on the detective.

"Can you tell me about your relationship with Oscar? I understand the two of you were close," she inquired, studying his face for any subtle reactions.

He swallowed hard, eyes darting nervously to his mother and back to Dory. He fidgeted with the edge of his apron as he struggled to find words. "We are. Oscar is my boyfriend, and we've been seeing each other for a while now."

"And does Adelaide know about your relationship?" Dory pressed, sensing there was more to the story.

Todd shook his head quickly, a flicker of fear crossing his features. His voice was full of anxiety. "We just kept it a secret until Oscar was ready to tell her."

Peg reached out to squeeze her son's shoulder, a look of pain across her features. "We're all just trying to get through this, Detective," she said wistfully, voice thick with emotion. "Hoping and praying that Oscar comes home safe. It's been so hard on all of us. You know, Todd's only a couple of years younger than the twins. They practically grew up together. It's made this whole situation even more complicated."

Dory acknowledged them with a nod and closed her notebook. "I understand. This is a difficult time for everyone involved. Thank you both for your time."

As she turned to leave, Todd's voice called out, halting her steps. "Wait, Detective," he said, his voice wavering uncertainly. "There's something else you should see."

The detective turned just in time to see Todd reach under the counter and pull out a worn leather-bound journal. He held it out to her, his expression reluctant yet determined.

"I found this when I was cleaning out some of Oscar's things," he said, his voice tense. "It's Ella's old diary from when she was in junior high, I think? I didn't read much, but what I saw worried me."

Dory took the diary gently from his hands, furrowing a brow as she flipped through the pages. Skimming the entries, specific passages caught her eye, the words leaping off the page with startling intensity.

I'll hate him for as long as I live, one entry read, the aged ink smudged and blotted with what looked like tears. *Oscar always gets everything he wants, and I'm left with nothing. It's not fair. Sometimes, I wish he would just go away.*

Dory's stomach lurched, a cold dread settling in her stomach. She had seen cases like this where a sibling rivalry had turned deadly.

Todd shifted uncomfortably as her eyes darted along the page. He averted his attention to the floor. "I just thought it may be important. With Oscar missing and everything that happened... Ella didn't always have the nicest things to say about him."

"Thank you, Todd. I appreciate that you brought this to my attention."

She turned to leave, journal in hand. Her thoughts already swirled with the possible meaning of what she'd just read—what it meant for the case. Suppose Ella's resentment of her brother had carried over into adulthood. Could it have played a role in his disappearance?

It was a disturbing thought, and one that Dory knew had to be explored further.

Chapter 5

Adelaide sprawled out on the bed, skin glistening with a sheen of sweat. She drew lazy circles on Frank's chest, his heart still pounding beneath her fingertips. The musky scent of their lovemaking lingered in the air.

"Ella was talking to that homeless guy," Adelaide said. "The one always hanging around the neighborhood, muttering to himself and rummaging through trash cans."

Frank grunted with his eyes half-closed. The weight of exhaustion was evident in his features, and he hardly mustered enough energy to engage in the conversation. "What about him?"

"He told her he was sorry. Sorry, Oscar's gone." Her fingers stilled along his chest, and a breath caught in her throat. "Like he knows something, Frank. Like he's privy to information, and we're not."

Frank's eyes snapped open, suddenly alert. He sat up abruptly, distancing Adelaide's hand from his chest. "What's that supposed to mean?" His voice was rough with agitation and fear. "Is he saying Oscar's dead? Is that what you're getting at?"

Adelaide shrugged, a deep frown tugging at her lips. "I don't know, Frank. I don't know anymore. Ella's got it in her head that people experiencing homelessness are tuned into some spirit world or something. Like they have a direct line to God, the universe, or whatever's out there."

Frank snorted. "That's ridiculous. It's nothing but superstitious nonsense."

"Is it?" Adelaide's look was sharp and searching, her gaze boring into Frank with an intensity that made him shift uncomfortably. "What if he knows something? What if Oscar is dead and trying to reach out to us? This is the sign we've been waiting for all along."

Frank's jaw clenched as he looked away, keeping his eyes fixed on the peeling wallpaper. "Oscar's not gone, Adelaide. Don't talk like that."

She sat up and pulled the sheet around her. "I'm not giving up on him, Frank. But what if something terrible has happened? I have to come to terms with it sooner than later."

Frank sighed with slumped shoulders. He reached out, one calloused hand cupping her face. "I know, baby. But turning him into a ghost won't help bring him back."

Adelaide leaned into his touch, eyes softly closed. His presence and solid warmth comforted her, serving as an anchor to the moment at hand.

"I should go," she said dryly. "Ella will be home soon."

She reached for some of her clothes that were scattered on the floor. Frank watched her dress, a heaviness settling in his chest. He knew there was nothing he could say to ease her pain or to fill the void left by her son's absence.

When Ella returned home from her shift at the coffeehouse, the apartment was strangely quiet. The usual sounds of her mother puttering around in the kitchen or Iris's gentle scampering were absent from the space. She frowned with unease, hanging her coat up on the wall.

"Iris?" she called, voice echoing against every corner of the apartment. "Where are you, baby?"

There was no response, just the low hum of the refrigerator and the sound of traffic on the street below. A knot of worry tightened in her stomach. She listened intently, hoping to hear the familiar pitter-patter of her paws.

It wasn't like Iris to avoid Ella's voice—she often eagerly awaited her return home, greeting her at the door with soft purrs. Something was wrong, and she could feel it in her bones. Her mind raced with possibilities.

She searched the apartment, looking under the bed, behind the curtains, and in all of Iris's favorite hiding places. Still, there was no sign of her beloved cat. With each passing moment, Ella's anxiety grew as worst-case scenarios played out in her mind.

She checked the windows, making sure they were all closed and secure, her heart pounding with each empty room she encountered.

"Iris!" she shouted desperately. "Come to Mommy!"

She sunk onto the couch, burying her face in her hands as a wave of despair washed over her. The apartment felt emptier than ever, the absence of Iris's presence magnifying the loneliness that had crept into her since Oscar's disappearance. She took a deep breath, trying to calm herself and think rationally about where she could be.

Suddenly, a soft, familiar sound caught her attention: the twinkling of Iris's collar coming from the front door. A surge of relief passed through her.

Ella raced forward and slung the door open, incredibly relieved to see that Iris was halfway between the rickety elevator and the apartment door, scampering toward her.

"Oh, my God," Ella breathed, dropping to her knees and scooping the cat into her arms, feeling the warmth of her tiny body against her chest. "You scared me half to death. Where have you been?"

As she held Iris against her, the cat began to make an odd choking noise. Ella pulled back, startled, just as Iris heaved and spat something onto the floor with a wet, sickening plop.

"Iris! What on earth—" Ella began, but her words faltered, eyes falling wide open at the object the cat had regurgitated.

It was Oscar's watch, the one he wore nearly every day for as long as she could remember. It was tattered, and the torn leather strap was frayed, bearing the marks of time and wear, but there was no mistaking its identity.

Her breath caught in her throat as she reached out with a shaking hand to pick it up, her fingertips brushing against the cool, saliva-coated metal surface.

The watch was now scratched and dirty, its face cracked, and its hands frozen at 11:13. She stared at it, her anxious mind already racing with questions. How did Iris get this? Could this somehow help lead her to Oscar?

With the slimy watch clutched in one hand and Iris tucked securely under her other arm, she hurried back into the apartment.

She sat the cat down safely and began to turn the watch around in her hands, examining it for clues. There was a small engraving on the underside of the watch face, a date Ella recognized as their shared birthday, and something else on the torn strap—something dark that stained the leather. Was it blood?

Tears stung the corners of her eyes as memories flooded back. The day she gave Oscar the watch, his face lit up with joy and surprise. It had been a symbol of their bond. Now, it could only be a timestamp of his disappearance and a piece of possible evidence.

Ella buried her face in the cat's soft fur. "Thank you, Iris," she whispered. "Thank you for bringing this to me. You're such a good girl."

A sharp knock on the door jolted her from her reverie. Iris leaped from her arms as Ella hurried to answer it.

She was surprised to see Detective Dingess standing there; her face grave and her eyes shadowed with what looked like pity.

"Detective," she said, her throat constricting with sudden fear. "What can I do for you?"

Ella's fingers tightened on the doorknob, bracing herself for whatever news the detective might bring.

Detective Dingess stood in the doorway, her posture rigid and her expression somber. "May I come in, Ella?"

Ella nodded, stepping back to allow the detective space to enter. Her heart thrummed tightly in her chest, a mixture of dread and anticipation coursing through her veins. She clutched Oscar's watch tightly, the cool metal digging into her palm.

As Dory stepped inside, her keen eyes swept the apartment, taking in every detail that seemed out of place. But, most importantly, she noticed the tension in Ella's shoulders, the way her fingers curled protectively around something in her hand.

"Is everything alright?" she asked, gaze settled on Ella's closed fist.

"Detective, something... strange happened just before you arrived," Ella confided, voice trembling slightly. She slowly opened her hand, revealing the battered watch. "My cat, Iris... she brought this home. It's *Oscar's* watch."

Dory's eyebrows shot up by a fraction, her professional demeanor momentarily slipping to reveal genuine surprise. She stepped closer, regarding the timepiece, with careful curiosity.

"May I?" She reached out a hand.

Ella nodded, reluctantly placing the watch in the detective's palm. She watched her scrutinize it, turning it over and studying the cracked face and torn strap.

"This could be important evidence, Ella," Dory said, her voice low and serious as she further examined it, hardly making eye contact. "I'm going to need to take this with me. Can you tell me exactly where your cat found it?"

Ella shook her head, slight frustration washing over her. "N-no. Iris got out of the apartment somehow for a while, and then she returned with it. I have no idea where she went to get it. I'm not even sure how she escaped."

Dory hummed thoughtfully. "I see. Well, this is certainly an interesting development." She carefully placed the watch in an evidence bag she produced from her pocket.

They ended up settling into two chairs at the worn kitchen table. Ella gave a few pleasantries, and Dingess pulled out a pen and notepad, ready to begin asking questions.

But just as she opened her mouth to speak, the sound of keys jingling outside the front door interrupted her. The door swung open, and they both turned to reveal Adelaide stumbling in, hair disheveled, and her clothes rumpled. She froze in the doorway as she took in the scene before her.

"What's going on here?" Adelaide asked, her gaze darting between Ella and the detective. The smell of stale cigarette smoke and cheap whiskey clung to her, a telltale sign of where she'd been.

Detective Dingess straightened her posture, her professional demeanor slipping back into place. "Mrs. Young, I'm glad you're here. There's something I have to tell both of you."

Adelaide stepped inside, closing the door behind her with a loud click. Her eyes narrowed as she studied the detective's face, somewhat suspicious. "Okay…"

Ella glanced at her mother, noticing the slight sway when she walked and the glassy look in her eyes. It was clear she had been drinking, seeking solace in the bottom of a bottle—and probably Frank's presence.

"I think you better sit down," Dory suggested, using a purposefully soft tone. "It's important."

"What is it?" Adelaide asked. "Is it Oscar? Have you found something?"

Detective Dingess gave both of them a somber expression. She took a deep breath, steeling herself for the difficult news she must deliver.

"I'm afraid it will be troubling," she began steadily despite the content of her words. "But a body has been found on the shoreline of Staten Island. It's a male, but we can't be sure of who it is yet. I wanted you to hear it from me first. There's a chance it may be an Oscar."

Adelaide's hand flew to her mouth, a strangled and guttural gasp escaping her lips. Ella's eyes widened in shock; her body froze in pure fear.

"What? You're serious?" Adelaide choked out.

Dory hesitated for a moment, choosing her words carefully. "The cause of death appears to be consistent with a suicide jump from the Verrazano Bridge. The body is crushed beyond recognition. We'll have to run a DNA test to confirm the identity, but the height and build match Oscar's description."

Ella felt as if she was going to be sick, her stomach churning with a sickening combination of grief and horror. She heard her mother let out a low, anguished groan at her side, her hands flying up to cover her face as she rocked back and forth.

Neither of them could believe it—they couldn't wrap their heads around the idea that Oscar was able to take his own life in such a horrific way.

But Ella knew it wasn't true even as the thought crossed her mind. Their Oscar would never do such a thing, not in a million years.

"No," she said fiercely, desperate her uncertain mind. "No, it's not possible! Oscar would never jump off a bridge. He wasn't suicidal, he wasn't... no, he would never do something like that."

The detective softened, her eyes glimmering with a sad, knowing look. "I know it's hard to accept," she began. "But sometimes, people can struggle with things we never even realize. Things they keep hidden, even from the people they love the most."

Ella shook her head. "No," she said again, her voice rising with emotion, nearly offended that the detective would further push the idea. "No, I don't believe it. Oscar would've told me if he was having problems. There must be another explanation! There must be something we're missing."

Adelaide seemed to struggle as she spoke. "I noticed some changes in his behavior before...

everything," she admitted, eyes glossy. "He seemed more withdrawn, more secretive."

"I understand this is a lot to take in," Dory said. "But we have to consider all possibilities, even the ones that are hard to face."

Ella felt like she had been stabbed in the gut, her world tilting off its axis. Could it be true? Could her brother have been so desperate, so hopeless, that he would take his own life?

"No," she said firmly, pushing the thought away out loud. "I don't believe it. I can't believe it. Oscar wouldn't do this to us, to me."

Adelaide's brow furrowed as she spoke, her voice tinged with frustration. "I don't know, Ella. You don't know. I just have this feeling in my gut that something wasn't right with Oscar. That he was struggling with something he couldn't talk about."

"What do you mean, Mom? You think Oscar was depressed? Why didn't you say anything before?"

Adelaide sighed heavily, her posture rigid. "It was little things. He would disappear for hours and come home with this... haunted look in his eyes. He would just shut down and refuse to talk when I asked him about it. It was like trying to break through a wall he'd built."

As her mother spoke, Ella's mind reeled. She wondered how she didn't see it. *How could she have been so blind to Oscar's suffering?*

Ella's voice cracked with emotion, barely audible even with the heavy silence of the room. She blinked rapidly, desperately holding back the tears that threatened to spill down her cheeks. "I had no idea... I thought he was happy." Her throat constricted around the words as if they were physically painful to speak out loud.

"I thought he was okay," she continued. "We shared everything. Or, I thought we did. How could I have missed something so important?"

She felt as though she had failed both Oscar and herself, questioning every moment they shared in recent memories.

Adelaide took her hand, fingers cold and trembling. "I know, baby. I thought the same thing. But sometimes people are good at hiding their pain, putting on a brave face for the people they love."

Ella was somewhat comforted by her mother's touch but felt a wave of guilt and shame wash over her, the emotions still crashing through her body like a tidal wave. She should have seen it. She should have known that something was wrong—that Oscar was in trouble. The signs must have been hidden beneath the surface of their seemingly everyday interactions for who knows how long, but she had been blind to them.

But she had been too wrapped up in her own life and focused on her problems to see the warning signs. So preoccupied with her job, relationship, and plans, leaving little room to notice the subtle shifts in Oscar's behavior. And now... now, it was too late.

"I'm so sorry, Mom. I'm so sorry I wasn't there for him." The words felt inadequate, unable to convey the depth of her regret and the weight of her failure. Ella's eyes stung with unshed tears as she grappled with the enormity of the occurrence.

Detective Dingess hesitated, not wanting to add more hurt to the already emotional room. "This doesn't end the investigation. There were signs of trauma to the body. We're working to piece together what happened in the days leading up to his disappearance."

"When will you know for sure?" asked Adelaide.

"We are expediting the DNA testing," she assured. "We should have the results within 24 to 48 hours. In the meantime, I know this is a challenging time for all of you. Please know that we are here to support you in any way we can."

Adelaide nodded as she wept, shoulders shaking unevenly. Ella felt a numbness settling over her, a cold emptiness threatening to consume her entire mind. The reality of the situation sank in, leaving her feeling hollow and disconnected from the world around her. She could only reach out and pat her mother on the shoulder as she sobbed.

Ella lay curled up on her bed. Lines of tears had long since dried on her cheeks, leaving behind a hollow ache in her chest that seemed only to expand. She stared blankly at the wall and ruminated.

She knew the detectives would leave no stone unturned, digging into every aspect of Oscar's life—and, by extension, her own. Secrets she'd kept buried for years, hidden away in the darkest corners of her mind, now threatened to resurface. Memories of a painful past she'd tried so desperately to escape now loomed darkly on the horizon like a gathering storm.

Her breath came in short, shallow gasps as she imagined the questions they would ask, the truths they would uncover. Her heart pounded against her ribcage as if trying to break free. She'd spent so long running from the ghosts of her past, constructing careful and pristinely kept barriers.

When would they be torn down?

Chapter 6

Adelaide sat at the kitchen table, hands wrapped around a mug of now-cold coffee. Frank leaned against the counter with his arms crossed over his chest. The kitchen remained eerily quiet.

"I just can't believe he might be gone," Adelaide whispered inaudibly. "Oscar was always so full of life, so alive. Could he really have done this to himself?" Her eyes, red-rimmed from countless hours of crying, searched Frank's face for answers she knew he couldn't provide.

Frank sighed heavily and pushed himself off the counter to sit beside her. He took her hand. "Sometimes people are hurting in ways we can't see," he said gently, his voice tinged with a sadness that hinted he was speaking from personal experience.

"Oscar was dealing with a lot—his sexuality, his relationship with Todd, the pressure of keeping it all a secret. Maybe it just got to be too much for him." Frank paused, swallowing hard. "Sometimes the weight of secrets can crush even the strongest spirits."

Adelaide nodded, fresh tears in her eyes. "If only I had seen it... I'm his mother. I should've known if he was struggling."

Frank squeezed her hand, his own eyes glistening. "You can't blame yourself, Adelaide. Oscar made his own choices. He knew he had people who loved him and would've supported him no matter what. But sometimes the pain is just too much to bear." He took a deep breath, his chest rising and falling with the effort. "We have to hold onto hope, but we also need to prepare ourselves for whatever the outcome might be."

Adelaide sighed, the reality of his words sinking in. As much as she wanted to believe that Oscar was still alive, she knew that every passing day made that hope a little dimmer. The thought scared her like nothing else.

"I just wish we knew something for certain, Frank. This waiting, this uncertainty… it's tearing me apart."

He nodded, pulling her into a tight embrace. "I know." His breath was warm against her ear. "Whatever happens, whatever we find out, we'll face it together."

Adelaide clung to him, her face buried in his shoulder as she cried. She knew the road ahead would be long and painful, filled with uncertainty and drawbacks—but with Frank at her side, she could only hope that he was able to lend her strength to endure whatever could come next.

Dory sank into her couch, exhaustion wracking her entire body. The case had consumed nearly every waking moment of her life, but the brief respite at home felt like a luxury. Just as she was able to close her eyes, the phone buzzed loudly with a call from the coroner's office.

"Detective Dingess," she answered, voice betraying her tiredness.

The voice on the other end was somber but measured with professionalism. "We have some new findings on the body believed to be Oscar Young's."

She sat up straight and rigid, adrenaline abruptly coursing through her veins with the prospect of more information. "What is it?"

"Not only has the body been positively identified as that of Oscar Young, but the crushing injuries sustained by the body," there was a pause and some slight shuffling on the other end as if the coroner were choosing his words carefully, "they occurred postmortem."

Dory felt a chill run down her spine as the implications sank in. Her years of experience told her that the case had just turned sinister. "So, you're saying..." she trailed off, needing to hear the words out loud.

"Yes. Oscar Young was already dead when he sustained the crushing injuries from the fall." His voice was heavy as he confirmed it. The silence that followed was thick with unspoken questions and the grim reality of what the investigation would have to endure.

Dory shook her head. The weight of this new information settled heavily on her shoulders, already tense from sleepless nights. If Oscar was already dead when he fell from the bridge, then that meant that his death wasn't a suicide.

Someone staged the scene to make it look like he had taken his own life.

The thought made her shiver. A sudden, terrible anger welled up inside her. Who could have done such a thing, and why? What motive could they have to murder an innocent young man?

"I'm sorry, Detective. I know this isn't the news you were hoping for." The coroner held a sympathetic tone, snapping Dory from her thoughts.

"It's fine, but you are certain about this?"

"Absolutely." His tone left no room for doubt. "The crushing injuries are very distinct from the other wounds on the body. There's no question that they occurred after death. The pattern of bruising and tissue damage is unmistakable…"

Dory took a deep breath. She ran a hand through her short-cropped hair, a nervous habit she had developed when processing complex information at work.

"Thank you for letting me know," she said gratefully despite the turmoil in her mind. "This changes everything. We're dealing with a calculated murder and a cover-up."

Her mind already started to plan a fresh approach to the case. She knew she had to inform her team, re-interview witnesses, and dig deeper into Oscar's life. The young man's secrets, including his recent coming out and relationship with Todd, suddenly became even more significant in light of the situation.

She needed to talk to Ella and Adelaide to see if they could shed any light on who may have had a motive to harm Oscar. Not only that, but she could picture their emotional faces: the sheer hurt of losing someone dear to them. Breaking the news to a family is never easy.

But first—a moment alone. A moment to process the news, a moment to let the reality of the murder settle down in her thoughts.

Chapter 7

Ella paced through the living room, nerves frayed as she and her mother waited impatiently for Detective Dingess' arrival. Adelaide sat on the couch, tapping her fingers to an anxious rhythm on her knee.

"This doesn't make sense," Ella groaned to no one in particular. She paced around, trying to piece together the fragments of information they had received. "Oscar couldn't have..."

She cut herself off, unable to even say the words out loud. Just the thought of her brother taking his own life felt like an immense betrayal.

Adelaide nodded, drawn and pale, the lines around her eyes deepening with worry. "I know, sweetheart. It's hard to believe."

Ella whirled around to face her mother. "Don't you think he would have at least left us a suicide note, some kind of explanation?" She raised her voice, echoing in the tense silence of the room. "Oscar wouldn't just... leave us like that. Without a word."

"Ella, please," her mother pleaded. "We don't know what she's found."

The shrill ring of the doorbell cut through their words, and they jumped in surprise. Ella gazed at her mother, scrambling to answer the door.

Detective Dingess stood on the other side, her posture rigid with the weight of the news she carried. "Ella," she began, her voice solemn. "May I come in?"

She stepped back wordlessly, her hand trembling on the doorknob. Dory walked past her and into the apartment with conviction. Every detail of the home stood out to her—the worn furniture with frayed edges and grey upholstery. This once-vibrant wallpaper now peeled at the corners, its pattern barely discernible beneath a layer of grime. Heavy sadness seemed to cling to every surface, telling a story of a family that had been torn apart.

As they all took a seat in the living room, they braced themselves for the worst. Ella's heart pounded so loudly she was sure the others could hear it. She knew, with a sinking certainty, that whatever the detective had to say would change their lives forever.

Dory leaned forward, her elbows on her knees, her face a mask of professional composure betrayed only by the sympathy in her eyes. "I'm afraid I have some difficult news to share with you both."

Ella's breath caught in her throat sharply in anticipation. She knew what was coming, in a sense. Her mother sank into the couch next to her, hands clenched into fists at her sides.

"The body that was found on the Staten Island shoreline," Dory paused, "has been positively identified as Oscar's."

Her eyes moved between the mother and daughter, witnessing the moment their world irrevocably changed.

Ella held her head in her hands, a strangled cry leaving her lips. Adelaide wrapped an arm around her, shoulders shaking wildly.

"I know this is tough to hear," Dory spoke compassionately, letting the weight of the moment settle, "but there is something else. Something that may make this even more difficult for both of you, and I'm sorry."

Adelaide looked up, eyes distraught and passionless like a caged animal. Her hand tightened around Ella's shoulder as she braced for the detective's words. "What is it?"

Dory hesitated; her brow tightened as she carefully mulled over her words. She could almost feel the weight of what she was about to reveal pressing down on her shoulders.

"The crushing injuries on Oscar's body are distinct from the other wounds. The forensic evidence is quite clear that they were sustained after death."

Adelaide's face visibly paled, and her lips trembled as she struggled to form a response. "What do you mean?"

Dingess inhaled, steeling herself for the impact. She leaned forward slightly as she spoke. "I'm not going to sugarcoat it... it means that someone staged the scene to make it look like Oscar had taken his own life. The evidence points to a deliberate attempt at misdirection. This could be a homicide."

The words hung in the air oppressively. Ella's hand flew to her mouth, eyes impossibly wide. Her fingers trembled against her lips, and for a moment, it seemed as though she might collapse.

"What?" Adelaide said, anger evident in her tone. "Who would do such a thing? Who could be so cruel?"

Dory remained impassive, but there was a flicker of something akin to anger in her eyes, a brief glimpse of the passion that drove her in her work.

"We're going to find out," she began, confidently slamming her pen on the table. "And I'm going to need your help."

Chapter 8

The soft glow of the desk lamp cast a warm, golden light over the pages of the diary, illuminating the faded ink and yellowing paper. Detective Dingess sat hunched over the desk; her brow furrowed in concentration as she carefully turned each page, scanning the looping, girlish handwriting for any clue.

At first glance, the diary seemed like any other, filled with an adolescent girl's complaints and concerns. There were entries about school, friends and enemies, the latest fashions, and celebrity crushes. Dory smiled at some innocent musings, remembering her teenage years with a mixture of nostalgia and relief that they were long behind her.

But as Dory read on, a darker picture emerged—one of a troubled, angry girl who harbored deep resentment toward her twin brother. The contrast between the light and dark entries was unsettling, like storm clouds gathering on a clear day. She grew increasingly uneasy as she delved deeper into the pages.

I hate him, one entry read. The ink was pressed deep into the paper as if the writer had channeled all her anger through the pen. *I hate how he always gets what he wants.* The intensity in the words made Dory's skin crawl, and she could almost feel the raw emotion emanating from the page. She wondered what incident had triggered such intense feelings.

Sometimes, I wish he would go away and never come back—a dark desire born from years of perceived injustice and sibling rivalry.

I wish I were an only child; another page opened with. *It's like I'm always in his shadow, no matter how hard I try.* She tried to imagine the constant comparison and competition that must have defined Ella's relationship with Oscar, sympathizing with a twin's struggle for individuality.

As she read on, she found herself torn between empathy for the young Ella's struggles and concern over the implications of the entries. She knew that teenage emotions could be a lot—often volatile and extreme. Still, she couldn't shake the feeling that these diary entries could be more than just typical sibling rivalry vented onto paper.

She flipped to another page, her eyes widening as she read the next entry, scribbled in with barely-legible impatience. *I had a dream last night. It was a dream where Oscar was gone, and I was the only one left. Everyone was so sad, so devastated... but I felt free like a weight had been lifted off my shoulders. Like I could finally breathe again.* The words seemed to leap off the page, each one a damning piece of evidence.

Dory's stomach churned roughly, a sickening realization dawning on her. Ella hadn't only resented her brother—she had wanted him gone, even dreamed of it. It was all so staggering.

She couldn't shake the feeling that there was more to the story than what met the eye, scouring every troubling entry with vigor. They all painted a picture of a relationship that spiraled out of control, and the world of hatred was slowly building up until... nothing. She flipped through the remaining pages frustratedly, but they were all blank. She sighed, left with more questions than answers.

She closed the journal with a soft thud and sat it on her cluttered desk, fingers lingering on its worn cover. Had Ella's jealousies persisted into adulthood, could they have boiled over into something more sinister? Could she have played a role in her brother's death, driven by a lifetime of pent-up anger and resentment?

Dingess sat at her desk, absently tapping her pen against her notepad in concentration. She tried to phone Ella earlier but never received an answer. Deciding to try another approach, she dialed Adelaide's number.

The phone rang several times before Adelaide picked up, her voice sounding tired but calm. "Hello?"

"Adelaide, it's Detective Dingess. How are you holding up?"

She sighed softly. "As well as can be expected. What can I do for you, Detective?"

"I was hoping to speak with Ella, but I haven't been able to reach her. Do you know where she is?

"Oh, she left a little while ago," Adelaide hummed. "Said she needed some air. I didn't ask where she was going, to be honest."

Dory nodded to herself, understanding the need for space during difficult times. "That's okay. I don't want to worry you, but if you see her, could you tell her I'd like to talk to her when she has a chance? It's about her diary."

"Her diary?" Adelaide echoed with a hint of curiosity. "How'd you come across that?"

"Todd gave it to me. He thought it might help with the investigation. There are some entries about Oscar that I'd like to discuss with Ella, but it's nothing urgent."

There was a long pause on the other end of the line. When Adelaide spoke again, her voice was thick with emotion. "Oh God," she whispered. "I remember those entries. I used to read Ella's diary when she was growing up. I know I shouldn't have, but..."

This unexpected revelation piqued the detective's interest. In an instant, she decided to press for more information gently. "What do you remember about these entries, Adelaide?"

She swallowed. "Ella wrote some terrible things about Oscar. She wished he would run away, or she would wish that she had been an only child... I always marked it up to be a normal sibling rivalry."

"Just have Ella call me if you see her," she dismissed calmly. "And Adelaide, take care of yourself, okay?"

"Thank you, Detective. I'll do my best," she said, voice somewhat warm.

As Dory hung up the phone, she leaned back in her chair, silently pondering the information from the diary. She knew she needed to talk to Ella soon—but it was equally important for the family to have space and time to process their grief.

She would wait for Ella to reach out by herself, knowing all too well that pushing too hard could lead to more harm than good.

The sky was a leaden gray, heavy with the promise of rain. Dingess ducked under the yellow crime scene tape that cordoned off the narrow alley. The air was thick with the stench of garbage and decay, and she had to breathe through her mouth to keep from growing nauseous.

She carefully picked her way through the debris that littered the ground, scanning the scene with her practical nature.

During the early hours of the morning, several units had been deployed to study the scene—a slouched body against a brick wall. A passing jogger had stumbled upon it, alerting many police and detectives.

The victim was a homeless man; his body sprawled awkwardly against the wall of the abandoned building that overlooked the alley. He was dressed in tattered, filthy clothes, his face obscured by a tangled mass of matted hair and a beard. The stench of decay caused everyone around to wrinkle their nose.

"What have we got?" Dory asked softly, turning to the officer who was dusting for fingerprints. She kept her voice steady, but an undercurrent of tension hid low in her stomach from the recent cases.

"Not much, I'm afraid," the officer sighed, tongue poking out in concentration as he applied powder to a nearby dumpster. "The victim's name is Bernard Martin. There are no obvious signs of a struggle, and the weapon appears to have been a blunt object. Probably struck from behind, given the position of the body."

"Anything else found at the scene?" she prompted as she crouched low to the ground. With precision, she swept her gaze around, looking for anything the others may have missed.

"A few personal effects, but nothing that seems immediately relevant to the case," the officer replied, straightening up and wiping his forehead with the back of his hand. "We're still combing through the evidence, but it's a pretty clean crime scene. Almost too clean, if you ask me."

Dory nodded in understanding, her lips pressed into a thin line. Something about this didn't sit right with her, but she couldn't pinpoint what it was. She stood up and brushed off her pants. Whatever happened here, she was determined to uncover the truth.

"Was there anything else found on the body?"

The officer shook his head, slight frustration in his eyes. "Just the usual personal effects—a few dollars in change, a lighter, an expired I.D. Nothing that screams evidence… you get it."

"Alright, officer, good work." Dory praised. She took a moment to study the scene before she paled, a horrible thought crossing her mind in a flash.

She crouched down beside the body, careful not to disturb the crime scene, her knees protesting the cold, hard ground. The man's eyes were open, staring blindly at the gray sky above, his weathered face frozen in surprise.

With a sickening lurch in her stomach, she realized that this was the homeless man who always hung around the neighborhood, his ragged figure a familiar sight to all nearby locals. He may have been the one—no, *he had to be the one* who'd given Ella that cryptic message about Oscar.

What would Bernard Martin's death mean if it were connected to Oscar Young's? Was the killer trying to silence him? Had he known or seen something that made him a target?

She stood up slowly, eyes never leaving the victim's face, as if all the answers would be revealed if she looked hard enough.

Chapter 9

The wind howled outside, rattling the windows and sending drops of rain crashing against the panes. Ella sat across from Peg at the coffeehouse, her hands wrapped around a steaming mug. The aroma of freshly brewed coffee and the chatter of the patrons filled the air, but Ella's focus remained solely on Peg.

"Todd gave your diary to Detective Dingess," she said measuredly. "He thought it might help with the investigation into Oscar's death. He believed there could be some... clues or information that would shed light on what happened to Oscar."

"He did what?" Ella's eyes widened, betrayed. She swallowed harshly, a look of pain evident on her face. *Todd*, her stepbrother, the person she thought she could trust—how could he do this to her? How could he expose her deepest, darkest thoughts without even giving her a chance to explain?

Peg reached across the table and placed a comforting hand over Ella's. "I know it's a lot to take in, but he was only trying to help. He's been struggling with everything, too, you know. He thought it would help the investigation."

Peg leaned back slightly, still attempting to soothe. "People go to great lengths to get answers, sometimes. We all want answers."

Ella shook her head vehemently and yanked away from Peg's touch. "But he had no right," she said, her words biting. "Those were my private entries, my secrets. Things I never intended for anyone else to see. How could he hand them over like that? Like they meant nothing?"

Peg sighed, her one good eye crinkling with sympathy. Her voice was soft now and almost pleading. "He didn't do it to hurt you, Ella. Everyone is just torn up. He thought it might give the detective some insight into your relationship with Oscar. Maybe something you wrote could shed light on where he might've gone, even."

Her words hung between them, a fragile attempt at building a bridge over the chasm of betrayal Ella was feeling.

But at the mention of her brother's name, Ella's face crumpled. Tears welled in her eyes as she thought about what she had written as a child and her resentment toward Oscar. The words she wrote in moments of frustration and jealousy, even wishing he had never been born, encouraged him to run away.

"They're going to think I had something to do with it," she whispered, her voice weak below the din of the coffeehouse. "They're going to read my entries and think I really wanted him gone. They'll see all those terrible things I wrote and assume the worst."

"They won't think that. You were just a child, Ella. You didn't mean those things. Siblings fight and say hurtful things all the time."

Despite the consolation, Ella couldn't shake the dread growing in the pit of her stomach. She knew the detective would read them and see a side of her she fought hard to hide. The words she penned in anger and frustration years ago would be brought to light, her darkest thoughts pulled word by word to be examined.

She couldn't help but think that it all came back to haunt her. That the secrets she'd kept hidden for so long would be the very things to tear her world apart...

Ella took a weak breath, her hands trembling as she set down her coffee cup with a light thud. "I was just a kid, Peg. I didn't mean those things. I never thought anyone would ever read those words."

"I know, honey. Kids say things they don't mean all the time. It's part of growing up."

Ella stared down at the table, tracing a fingernail across a worn grain of wood. "Oscar was a needy kid," she rushed out. "He always wanted all the attention. I got tired of having to share everything with him. It felt like I could never catch a break."

She took a long sip of her coffee to steady herself. "There were times I wished I was an only child," Ella admitted as the cup settled back onto the table. "I know it's awful to say, but I just wanted some space, some time to myself. To figure out who I was without being part of a pair."

"It's okay to feel that way," Peg spoke gently. "Siblings can be a lot to deal with, especially when you're young. It doesn't make you a bad person to have wanted some independence. It makes you human."

Ella nodded, a tear sliding down her cheek. "I loved Oscar." Her voice broke. "I never really wanted anything bad to happen to him. But those words—the things I wrote—make it seem like I did."

Peg nodded. "Detective Dorianne will understand. She'll see that you were just a girl working out your feelings in the only way that you knew how to."

"I hope so. I don't know what I'll do if they think I had something to do with Oscar's death."

Peg leaned in closer. "We would face it together." Her voice was filled with much more conviction than Ella's. "You'll always have me on your side. We've been through our share of tough times. We can get through this, too."

Ella gave a small, unsure smile in return.

Adelaide strode into the coffeehouse, rain-soaked, the bell over the door ringing out. Peg looked up from behind the counter, her expression hardening at the sight.

"We're closed," Peg said dryly, not bothering to look any longer. She continued to wipe down the counter, movements slow and methodical.

Adelaide lifted an eyebrow, a smirk playing at the corners of her mouth. Her glassy eyes, sharp and calculating, scanned the coffeehouse. "Oh, funny."

Sensing the tension between the two women, Ella quickly rose from her seat. "Come on in," she defused. "She's kidding."

But Peg's look said otherwise. Her jaw clenched as Adelaide approached the table where Ella was sitting. The air was thick with unspoken hatred, years of resentment and bitterness between them that only grew more tense with the shared grief.

Adelaide pulled out a chair, its legs scraping the tiled floor with a harsh sound that echoed on every wall of the coffeehouse. She sat down with a heavy, unstable thud. "I need to talk to you."

She nodded and sank back into her seat with slumped shoulders. She could feel Peg's stare, unsettling and intense, watching every move like a protective hawk.

"So, what's wrong?" Ella asked. She could tell her mother had been drinking; the faint smell of alcohol clung to her, and her words nearly slurred together.

Adelaide leaned forward, elbows on the table. "I heard from a regular at O'Malley's." She fixed Ella with an intense stare that made her want to shrink away. "He said that Oscar was involved with some drug dealer before he died. That he saw them together more than once."

Her mouth fell open in shock. "What?" Her voice trembled with disbelief. "That can't be true. Oscar would never... he wasn't into drugs." She shook her head vehemently as if trying to reject her mother's words physically.

Adelaide's shoulders fell uncertainly. "We don't know," she admitted. "It could just be some barroom gossip. But it got me thinking... what if they're behind what happened to Oscar?"

She thought back to the last few months of Oscar's life, trying to remember if there were any signs he was in trouble. But nothing came to mind.

"Did you tell the detective?" Ella asked, trembling with trepidation.

Her mother shook her head, lips pressed into a thin line. "No. I wanted to talk to you first. I don't know if it's even worth mentioning."

Ella sat up straighter, her eyes wide with urgency. "It is worth mentioning. We have to tell her. Even if it's just a rumor, it could be important. We can't afford to overlook anything when it comes to this."

Adelaide nodded grimly. "You're right." The words came out slowly as if she was hesitant to admit it. "We can't just keep it to ourselves. Not when it can help discover what may've happened to him."

But her eyes grew narrow as she continued, her voice taking on an accusatory, razor-sharp edge. "By the way," she tapped a finger on the wooden surface of the table. "I heard about the diary from Detective Dingess. She said Todd gave it to her, that there were entries about Oscar."

Ella felt her heart plummet. She knew this moment would come, but she hoped to have more time to prepare, to find the right words to explain. "Mom, I..."

Adelaide swiftly silenced her with a raised hand, eyes flashing with anger and disbelief.

"What were you thinking, Ella?" she snapped. "Writing those things about your brother, about wishing he would disappear?"

She flinched visibly at the accusation, arms crossed wearily to shield herself from the onslaught of her mother's words. "I was only a child. I didn't mean it, I swear. It was just... just silly thoughts, nothing more."

She looked up at her mother, silently pleading for understanding—pleading for forgiveness. The young girl who wrote those careless words had no way of knowing the weight they would, one day, carry.

But Adelaide wasn't listening. She only leaned forward, voice dropping with suspicion. "I'm beginning to think you might have hurt him. You wrote about it in your diary?"

Shock and horror etched along Ella's face. "No!" She cried out. "I would never hurt Oscar. You know that!"

Adelaide scoffed and shook her head, her lips curling into a sneer. "Do I?" she asked, though it was more of an accusation. "'Cause from where I'm sitting, you wanted him gone. You resented him so much that you were willing to do anything to get rid of him. All those little fights, all those jealous moments... they add up, don't they?"

Ella felt like she couldn't breathe, the weight of her mother's accusations pressing down on her chest. The room seemed to spin around her, and she grasped the table's edge harshly to steady herself.

"Please," Ella pleaded, tears endlessly falling down her cheeks. Her voice grew small again. "You have got to believe me. I loved Oscar so much. I never wanted anything bad to happen to him. We had our moments, sure, but he was my brother, my best friend. How can you even think that about me?"

Adelaide stood abruptly, her chair scraping against the floor. "You'll never understand what it's like," she said, her voice sharp like a dagger, "to lose a child, to have that hole in your heart that can never be filled."

She looked down at Ella, her expression twisting into something cruel and unrecognizable. "And you never will."

Ella flinched. She knew what her mother implied, the secret she had carried for so long.

"Because you can't have children of your own."

Peg stepped forward, her hand placed on Ella's shoulder. "That's enough." Her one good eye narrowed dangerously at Adelaide. "You need to go. Now."

Adelaide looked at Peg, her brutal gaze full of adrenaline. "This isn't over," she promised. "I won't *rest* until I find out what happened to my son. And if Ella had anything to do with it, I'll make sure she pays."

With that, she turned on and stalked out of the coffeehouse.

Ella immediately collapsed back into her chair, her body shaking with wrecked sobs. Peg knelt at her side, wrapping an arm across her form.

"She's wrong," Peg's voice was soothing but imperative. "I know you didn't hurt Oscar. She just lashed out. It was the alcohol."

Ella rested her head down on the table for stability, eyes burning. She could only hope Peg was right about her mother.

Part Two

Chapter 10

As Oscar's wake began, Dory positioned herself strategically, watching the family members take their seats. She noticed the tension between Adelaide and Peg, how they sat on opposite sides of the room. Ella sat not far off, evidently guilty and nervous, sweeping her gaze across the room as if searching for something or someone.

Throughout the service, Dory remained vigilant, eyes and ears tuned to every detail. She listened methodically to the eulogies and watched each mourner's body language, looking for signs of deception.

Adelaide's face, a mask of detachment, seemed to drift into a world of her own, her eyes unfocused and her hands clasped tightly in her lap. The detective couldn't help but wonder what thoughts were churning behind her facade. Meanwhile, Peg sat ramrod straight, her single eye fixed on the proceedings with an unwavering intensity that spoke of steely determination or, perhaps, suppressed emotions.

Dingess made a series of mental notes as the service progressed, her investigative instincts on high alert. She resolved to keep an incredibly close eye on both women, watching for subtle inconsistencies in their behavior.

Ella stood beside the polished wooden casket, keeping her eyes fixed on the framed photograph of

Oscar that rested on the gleaming surface. His joyous face looked back at her, forever frozen in a moment of purity. Now, it all seemed like a cruel mockery of the harsh reality surrounding her. Soft murmurs of mourners filled the room, but she hardly registered their presence.

She felt a hand on her shoulder. "How are you holding up, honey?" Peg stood at her side, gentle and worried.

Ella swallowed hard, fighting back the lump in her throat. "I don't know. It doesn't feel real, you know? Like any minute, he will walk through that door and tell us it was all just a big misunderstanding," she admitted, drifting back to Oscar's photograph. "I keep expecting to hear his laugh, that mischievous glint in his eye."

Peg nodded, her eyes shimmering with sympathy. "I know. I keep expecting the same thing." She squeezed Ella's shoulder, offering what little comfort she could in the face of such overwhelming loss.

Peg glanced around the room, taking in the somber atmosphere and the hushed conversations. Adelaide stood by the coffin with a glazed, unfocused look, her hands trembling slightly at her sides. "Your mother, she's not well, is she?"

Ella shook her head, a bitter laugh escaping her lips. "That's an understatement. She's been drinking more than ever, and she won't even talk to me about what happened. It's like she's completely shut down."

Ella's eyes flickered to her mother, noting the way she swayed slightly on her feet. Peg sighed heavily, her presence comforting in the storm of emotions swirling around them.

"One day at a time," she said, voice low and determined.

Ella's chest grew tight, like a heavy weight pressing down on her lungs. She could feel the hot sting of tears behind her eyes, threatening to spill over at any moment.

She had to be strong and hold herself together for a little longer. The thought echoed in her mind like a mantra, a desperate plea to her resolve.

But as she stared down at Oscar's face in the photograph, at the hazel eyes that had always sparkled with laughter, she felt something inside her break. At that moment, his absence felt more palpable than ever, a gaping void that nothing could fill.

A soft, choked sound escaped her throat, and she put a hand to her mouth, trying to stifle the sob that threatened to break free. She couldn't face a world without her brother in it.

"Ella?" a soft voice murmured from behind her, and she felt a warm hand rest on her back. "Are you okay?"

She turned to see Todd, his usual confident demeanor replaced by a vulnerability she rarely witnessed. His eyes were red and puffy as if he had been crying, and his shoulders looked weighted.

For a moment, Ella felt gratitude towards him, appreciating his presence after so long. But then, just as quickly, the memories of the past few days came rushing back, and she felt a cold, hard knot of anger and betrayal settle in the pit of her stomach.

"How dare you, Todd." Her voice sounded brittle and on the verge of breaking. She shrugged off his hand with a sharp jerk, taking a deliberate step away. "How dare you betray me like that? I trusted you."

Todd's face fell into an expression of hurt and confusion. "Ella, I'm sorry. I really am. I thought I was doing the right thing. I never meant to hurt you."

"The right thing?" Ella scoffed, her words dripping with bitter sarcasm. "Giving my diary to that detective, revealing all my deepest, darkest secrets to a stranger? How could that possibly be the right thing? Do you have any idea how violated I feel?"

"I was just trying to help," Todd pleaded desperately. He ran a hand through the back of his hair. "Maybe there was something in there. Some clue that could help us find out what happened to Oscar."

Ella's jaw clenched tightly; her hands balled into fists at her sides. "Well, there wasn't," she spat out, her voice trembling with unconcealed feelings. "There was nothing in there that could be relevant to the investigation. Not a single thing. All you did was violate my privacy and make me look like a suspect in my brother's death. Do you have any idea how that feels?"

"I'm sorry," he whispered, his voice thick with regret. "I never wanted to hurt you. That was the last thing I ever intended. I loved him too, you know? Oscar meant the world to me. And I would do anything, anything at all, to bring him back. Can't you understand that?"

Ella's throat tightened, and a lump formed that she struggled to swallow. Her anger faded as quickly as it had come, leaving a hollow ache in her chest. Deep down, she knew Todd was hurting just as much as she was, that he had loved Oscar just as deeply, just as fiercely. The pain in his eyes mirrored her own, a shared grief that threatened to consume them both.

But despite this understanding, she couldn't forgive him. Not yet. The betrayal was too fresh, the wound too raw. Ella turned away, unable to bear the sight of Todd's pleading face any longer.

"I know. But it doesn't change what you've done, Todd. And I don't know if I can ever trust you again after this."

"I understand, Ella. And I'm sorry, sorrier than I could ever explain to you."

With that, she turned and walked off, leaving Todd standing alone. As he watched her disappear into the crowd, he couldn't help but wonder if he created an irreparable rift in their relationship.

As Ella passed by, Detective Dory gently touched her arm to grab her attention. "Ella, there's something I need to tell you."

"Yes, of course. What is it, Detective?" Ella attempted to sound genuine, putting the conversation with Todd behind her.

Detective Dory's eyes met Ella's, filled with professional detachment and genuine sympathy. She glanced around the room at the other mourners. "I know this isn't the right time or place," she began, voice low and serious, "but I thought you'd want to know as soon as possible."

Ella nodded, and Dingess exhaled softly before speaking again. "The lab results came back. They confirmed that the blood found on the watch was Oscar's."

"Oh no." Ella's face paled. "What does that mean?"

She chose her words carefully, and her expression was somber. "We're still investigating all possibilities. Nothing is certain yet. But I thought you'd want to know about this development right away. I know this is a lot to take in, especially right now."

"Thank you for telling me, Detective," she said, her voice steadier than what she felt inside.

Suddenly, Adelaide's piercing, anguished wail shattered the atmosphere of the wake. Ella and Dory quickly turned to see what was happening.

"No!" Adelaide cried out sharply. "Don't you dare try to comfort me, Peg! I won't have it!"

Peg recoiled as if she'd been physically struck. "Adelaide, I... I didn't mean to..."

The other mourners trailed off into a tense silence, their conversations dying as all eyes turned to the unfolding drama. Their faces wore a combination of unease and morbid curiosity. Sensing the escalating situation, Ella rushed to her mother's side. She put a gentle but firm hand on her shoulder, trying to calm her down.

Adelaide turned to Peg; her eyes narrowed into slits. Her voice trembled with rage. "This is all because of you," she spat. "You and your precious Todd. You let him hurt my Oscar! I'll never forgive you, Peg. Never!"

"Stop it, Mom," Ella interjected, embarrassed. "This isn't Peg's or Todd's fault, and you're making a scene!"

After a moment of silence, she glanced around apologetically at the stunned onlookers before grabbing Peg's clenched hand. "Come on, Peg. Let's get some fresh air."

Ella retreated to the sanctuary of her childhood bedroom and closed the door. She sank onto the edge of the bed, fingers trembling as she retrieved her phone and found her boyfriend's number in her contacts.

She held her breath, counting the rings, willing him to pick up. Sam's voice was warm and familiar when he finally answered, a balm to her frayed nerves. "Hi, honey," he said. "How are you holding up?"

At the sound of his voice, something inside her broke. All the pain, fear, and grief she had been holding in came pouring out, her words tumbling over each other in a desperate flood.

"Oh, Sam, it is so good to hear your voice," she choked, tears already welling up.

"Sweetheart, I'm so sorry I couldn't be there with you today." His voice was heavy. "I feel awful that I couldn't be by your side."

"I know, I understand. I just... I really needed you today, Sam. It was so hard being there without you."

"I can't imagine what you're going through right now, Ella. Losing Oscar, dealing with the investigation, your mom... it must be overwhelming. I'm so sorry you had to face the wake alone."

Ella was crying now, hot tears rolling down her face. "Everything is just so messed up. I don't know what to do. I feel so lost."

"Shh, honey. It's okay. You're not alone in this, I promise. I'm here for you, even if I couldn't be there today. We'll get through this together."

She took a shaky breath, attempting to steady herself. "There's something else, Sam. Todd... he gave the police my old diary from when Oscar and I were, like, kids. Now they're asking all these questions, digging into things I wrote years ago. I'm scared of what they'll think."

"What do you want to tell them?"

Ella closed her eyes, the tumultuous emotions threatening to overwhelm her. "The truth," she finally said. "But I'm afraid, Sam. Scared of what they'll think, what they'll do. Afraid they'll think I had something to do with Oscar's death."

Sam made a soothing sound, his voice warm and reassuring. "They're not going to blame you, Ella. You've done nothing wrong. You're a victim in this too; anyone who knows you will understand that."

Ella slowly relaxed as his words washed over her. "Thank you. I don't know what I'd do without you."

Her fingers tightened around the phone as she steeled herself for what she had to say next. "Sam. There's something else I wanted to tell you. Something important."

"Yeah, what is it?"

Ella swallowed hard. The words felt heavy on her tongue, but she forced them out. "I'm starting to think that Todd may have harmed Oscar," she confessed. "And it scares me even to consider it. This feeling has been gnawing at me for days..."

Relief and dread washed over her as the words hung in the air. She had finally given reprieve to the dark thoughts that had been plaguing her, but now that they were out in the open, they felt even more terrifying and real.

Chapter 11

Detective Dingess sat at her desk, poring over the forensic report on Oscar's death. She rubbed at her temple, trying to ease the throbbing pain that had settled behind her eyes.

One section in particular caught her eye as she flipped through the report. It was the DNA analysis, a routine part of any investigation, that often yielded crucial information. As she read over the results, a breath caught in her throat.

According to the report, Oscar's DNA was a 100% match to Ella's. It was not simply a close match as expected from siblings—it was an exact match that could only mean one thing. Oscar and Ella were *identical* twins.

Dory leaned back in her chair, recalling her interactions with Ella and how she had talked about her brother and their bond. The depth of their connection made sense now.

They were identical: two halves of the same whole, bound by a genetic code as unique as it was unbreakable.

But something else was nagging at the back of her mind, refusing to be ignored. If Oscar and Ella were identical twins, why hadn't anyone mentioned it? Why hadn't it come up in interviews with family and friends? The omission seemed too significant to be a mere oversight, and her instincts told her that there was more to the story than what met the eye.

Her mind raced as she recalled her earlier conversations with Ella and Adelaide, sifting through every word and gesture for clues she might have missed. In particular, one offhand remark had stuck in Dory's mind.

"That damned cat. I don't know why Ella always wanted one," Adelaide had muttered under her breath. "Guess she still does."

Dory had dismissed the comment as nothing more than an odd remark. But now, as she sat at her desk trying to piece together the jagged fragments of the case, the words took on a new meaning.

Identical twins *can't* be born of opposite sexes.

Were Ella and Oscar both born male? Had Ella undergone a transition to become female, or had it been Oscar?

Why had Ella never mentioned that she and Oscar were identical twins? What other secrets was she keeping? The questions gnawed at her mind, opening a Pandora's box of possibilities she hadn't previously thought about.

And most importantly, what did this mean for the investigation? Did Ella know more about Oscar's fate than she was letting on?

Another realization dawned on Dory, dots connecting forcefully in her mind. She straightened her shoulders, eyes widening at the notes below her. One thing became immediately clear.

The missing brother, the one the neighbors had mentioned, the one who had disappeared years ago...

He didn't disappear at all.

He became Ella.

The puzzle pieces fell into place, revealing a picture she hadn't expected.

At the center was the enigmatic figure of Ella Young, a woman whose true story remained shrouded in mystery.

Detective Dingess hesitated for a moment, finally dialing Adelaide's phone number. She drummed her fingers along the desk, patiently waiting for the ringing to stop.

Adelaide lay tangled in the sheets with Frank, the lampshade casting a yellow glow in the dim room. She silenced him with a finger to her lips, grabbing the buzzing phone on the nightstand.

"Hello?"

"Adelaide," Dory began, "I have some important information to share with you and Ella."

"What is it, Detective?" Adelaide sounded cautious, clutching the sheet tighter around her chest with her free hand.

She chose her words carefully. "The homeless man who gave Ella the message about Oscar—he was murdered."

Adelaide sat up quickly in bed, the blankets pooling at her sides. Frank watched her intently, his expression morphing from confusion to concern just as the color drained from her face.

Frank reached out to touch her arm, but she waved him off impatiently, inaudibly hissing some words before turning away. She tuned in to the detective, heart pounding.

"Murdered?" Adelaide echoed weakly. "What does this mean? Is it related to Oscar?"

"I'm not sure yet." Dory sighed. "There's something else I need to ask you that can help the investigation right now. It might be sensitive, but trust me, it is crucial."

Adelaide's mouth suddenly felt dry. She glanced nervously at Frank as if she could be consoled at a moment's notice.

"What is it?"

"I know that Oscar and Ella are identical twins," Dory said, her tone matter-of-fact. She offered a moment of quietness, checking for a reaction on the other end. "But I need to know... were they both born male or female? More specifically, was Ella born a boy or a girl?"

Adelaide felt her throat tighten as the detective awaited an answer. She glanced nervously at Frank, suddenly very aware of his presence. She didn't want to have this conversation in front of him.

"You should go," she said hurriedly. "I need to speak with the detective in private."

Frank opened his mouth as if to protest, but with one look at Adelaide, he nodded and left the bedroom with his clothes.

Once he was gone, Adelaide turned back to the phone with a heavy sigh. She spoke quickly, wincing. "Yes. Ella was born as Elliot. She transitioned to female."

The detective remained silent on the other end of the line, giving Adelaide a moment to collect herself. She could sense there was more to be said.

"It wasn't easy," Adelaide continued, her voice thick with emotion. "Oscar... he had a tough time accepting it at first. They were so close growing up. Ella's transition drove a wedge between them that I'm not sure they ever fully overcame."

Tears stung Adelaide's eyes as painful memories resurfaced. "Oscar lashed out and said terrible things he could never take back. Ella was strong through it all, but I know it deeply hurt her. There were nights I'd hear her crying alone in her room, and I just felt so helpless as a mother."

Dory made a note, her heart aching for the family's struggle. "Do you think that the rift between Oscar and Ella could have played a role in what eventually happened to him?" She asked the question gently, treading carefully on such sensitive ground.

Adelaide was silent for a long moment. "I don't know," she finally admitted. "But I can't help but wonder if things might have turned out differently if Oscar had been more accepting from the start. If he had just loved his twin like he always had, regardless of gender. The guilt... it eats at me sometimes."

Dory sighed appreciatively. "Thank you for sharing such a personal story, Adelaide. I know that couldn't have been easy."

After a quiet hum from Adelaide and soft static on the other end, the detective scribbled a few finishing words and closed her notebook with a soft thud. "I'll keep in touch, Adelaide."

Chapter 12

Detective Dingess entered the coffeehouse, spotting Ella behind the counter. Her hair was pulled back in a ponytail, and her soft features strained with the stress of the recent events.

Ella looked up as she approached, eyes wide with surprise. "Detective Dingess," she greeted, her voice kind despite unease. "How can I help you?"

Dory leaned against the counter with a serious expression, quiet and mindful of the other patrons. "Ella, we need to talk. Is there somewhere we can speak in private?"

"Okay," she whispered, glancing around the busy shop. "Just give me a minute to hand things over to my coworker."

Ella disappeared into the back room and returned a few moments later with her apron draped over her arm. "Let's go outside."

She led Dory through the shop and out to a quiet corner of the patio, the sun filtering through the changing leaves of a nearby tree. The crisp autumn air carried the faint scent of churning coffee and decadent sweets from the building.

Dory took a steady breath, her heart heavy with the news to deliver.

"Ella," she began, adjusting in her seat. "I'm afraid I have some news about the homeless man you spoke to that gave you that cryptic message. His body was found in an alley nearby, murdered. The details are... quite troubling."

Ella gripped the edge of the table. "Murdered?" She swallowed harshly. "Who could have done this?"

Her expression remained unreadable as she leaned forward. "We don't know yet. It's too early to say for sure, but the timing is certainly suspicious."

"What does this all mean?"

Dory sighed and ran a hand through her short blonde hair, a rare display of frustration breaking through her exterior. "It means we have to take a closer look at everything," she explained gravely. "The message he gave you, the circumstances around his death, could tie back to Oscar. We're not ruling anything out at this point."

"Do you think someone was trying to keep him quiet? Like they didn't want him to say something about Oscar?"

Dory's expression remained guarded. "I can't speculate on that right now, but I *can* tell you that this changes things. We must dig deeper and follow every lead, no matter how small." Her gaze softened in the direction of Ella. "And I'm a little concerned for your safety, too. Please be on the lookout and take precautions. I don't want anything to happen to you during this investigation."

Ella nodded warmly, but her throat felt tight. "Of course. I definitely will." She paused, glancing off, sensing there was more to be said. "Anything else?"

"Your mother mentioned that Oscar might have been involved with a drug dealer. Do you know anything about that?"

"No, that doesn't sound like him at all," she insisted, dismissing the notion with a wave of her hand. The idea of her brother being mixed up in anything dangerous seemed utterly impossible.

"What about Todd?" she asked softly, searching Ella's face. "They're both musicians. Sometimes, that scene involves recreational drugs. Did you ever notice anything?"

Ella remained silent for a moment as if searching her memory. Her mind combed through countless nights of concerts and late-night jam sessions, trying to recall anything particularly drug-related. "I don't know," she spoke defeatedly. "Oscar and Todd spent a lot of time together at gigs and rehearsals. I wasn't always there. They had their own world, in a way."

Ella's hands trembled. She set down her coffee cup, blowing at the steam rising from the freshly brewed coffee. She could feel the detective's stare, the weight of unasked questions hanging between them.

"Ella," Dory finally began, her voice somewhat firm. "I need to ask you something. It's about you and Oscar."

Ella's heart pounded in her chest. She could guess what was coming, but that didn't make it any easier to face. Her mouth went dry. She swallowed hard, attempting to maintain her composure.

"What about us?" she managed.

Dory chose her words carefully. "Ella, why didn't you tell me that you're transgender? And that you and Oscar were identical twins?"

Ella's heart pounded in her chest. "I... I'm not sure," Ella managed. "I guess I was worried about how you might react. It's not something I'm always comfortable sharing."

"Ella," Dingess interjected softly, "I need to understand everything about your relationship with

Oscar if I'm going to find out what happened to him. Every detail matters, no matter how small or personal."

Ella finally took a deep, shuddering breath, eyes rimmed with soft tears that she wiped away. "I'm sorry, Detective," she confessed. "I was afraid... afraid of how it might affect the investigation, afraid of being judged."

Detective Dingess nodded sympathetically as she absorbed Ella's words. "I understand your hesitation, but this information is crucial. I appreciate your honesty now. It helps me understand the situation better."

Ella nodded gratefully, and Dory leaned forward, her gaze intent and unwavering. "But there's more. I need to address something your mother mentioned. She seems to believe you might have had something to do with Oscar's death... that there was some tension between you, particularly regarding your transition. Can you tell me more about that?"

Ella closed her eyes, fresh tears spilling down her cheeks. Her voice quivered as she spoke. "My mother... she's not entirely wrong. Oscar was initially repulsed by the idea of his brother becoming his sister. It was a difficult time for both of us. But over time, he came to understand and even support me."

Detective Dingess's pen hovered over her notepad. "I have to be straight with you, Ella. From an investigative standpoint, you had a motive. The diary entries we found and the resentment you expressed towards Oscar are things we can't ignore."

Ella shook her head vehemently, voice growing flat. "You have to understand. Those entries were from years ago. I was just a confused, angry child then. I didn't know how to process my feelings."

Ella paused, pulling on the arm of her sweater. "Oscar and I were identical twins. We looked so much alike, and I... I hated it. Every time I saw him, it was like looking in a mirror. I hated seeing my face staring back at me, day after day."

Her voice dropped to a whisper, thick with emotion. "The self-loathing I felt was overwhelming. I was disgusted with myself—with the body I was trapped in. It wasn't Oscar I resented. It was the constant reminder of who I was trying so hard not to be." She sighed, newfound clarity in her voice. "But I would never, *ever* have hurt my brother. No matter how much pain I was in."

But Dory leaned forward, her piercing gaze fixed on Ella as she spoke. "I don't think your mother would just say that without reason. If you were involved in Oscar's death, did someone help you move his body? Did the homeless man help you?"

Ella's breath caught in her throat, and she angled her body away instinctively as if she were distancing herself from the accusation. "What? Oh my God, you've got to be kidding me!"

"The homeless man died before I could even question him," Dory continued, her tone matter-of-fact. "I think someone wanted him silenced. It's too convenient, don't you think?"

"Oh please," she retorted, a hint of anger creeping into her voice. "Do you honestly think I would tell you about the cryptic message he gave me about Oscar if he was my accomplice? That doesn't make any sense."

Dory's eyes narrowed, and she cocked her head to the side, studying Ella's face intently. "Ella," she said, her voice taking on a gentler tone, "I have to ask these questions. It's my job. I must explore every possibility, no matter how unlikely. You understand that, don't you?"

The detective then leaned back in her chair, her fingers steepled under her chin. "If you and Oscar were identical... wouldn't that mean he was struggling with the same feelings you were?" she probed gently. "The same feeling of being trapped in the wrong body?"

"No, Detective. That's not how it works," she explained, exasperated. "Just because we share the same DNA doesn't mean we share the same identity or sense of self. We may have looked alike, but we are two distinct individuals."

She took a deep breath, her eyes fixed on a spot just over Dory's shoulder. "Oscar was gay, Detective. It took him a long time to accept and come to terms with that. He was so afraid of what people would think and how they would judge him. But his relationship with Todd helped him be more open about it, to embrace who he truly was."

"I had nothing to do with Oscar's death," she continued, her voice steady despite the tumultuous emotions swirling inside her. A beat passed, and then she added: "But there's someone you should investigate. Todd."

Dory raised an eyebrow, her interest visibly piqued. "Todd? Your stepbrother?" she asked. "What makes you think he might be involved?"

Ella's voice quivered as she spoke, her eyes unfocused and distant, as if lost in a tangle of painful memories. "Todd had feelings for me when I was a boy, but I couldn't reciprocate them. It was too complicated, too messy. I was going through a lot. We were family, if not by blood. The whole situation made me uncomfortable."

"And when you transitioned?" the detective prompted.

"That's when everything changed," Ella replied. "Suddenly, Todd's affections shifted to Oscar. It was like he was replacing me with a carbon copy. I saw the way he looked at him, the way he sought out his company. It was disturbing."

She paused, swallowing hard before continuing. "But it was never the same. Oscar was his own person. He could never be me, no matter how much Todd might have wanted him to be. I think that frustrated Todd, maybe even angered him."

"Ella," Dory said quietly, "I know this is hard, but I must ask. Do you think Todd could have had something to do with Oscar's death?"

Ella's eyes snapped up to meet Dory's, a flicker of something dark and haunted crossing her face. "I don't know," she admitted. "But there's something else you should know about Todd. Something that might be important."

Dory studied Ella's face intently. "I'm listening."

Ella hesitated for a moment. She knew that what she was about to say would change everything, that it would shatter the fragile peace that settled over their family in the wake of Oscar's death.

Her voice finally dropped to a whisper. "He's the one who caused Peg to lose an eye. It happened about a year after my father passed away. Todd was devastated by his death, of course, but he took it harder than anyone expected."

She paused, swallowing hard. "When he found out Peg was seeing someone new, he just couldn't handle it. Todd didn't want her to move on. He saw it as a betrayal of my father's memory." Ella's hands trembled slightly as she recalled the incident. "That's when he lashed out and stabbed Peg in the eye in a moment of blind rage."

Dory's eyebrows shot up. "What are you talking about, Ella? What did Todd do?"

"I don't remember exactly what happened," she confessed wearily. "But I know Todd had been drinking and that he was angry. He started throwing things, smashing bottles and plates against the walls."

Dory's eyes widened in shock, her pen scratching furiously across the page as she absorbed the details. "And Peg? What happened to her?"

Ella's face crumpled. "She tried to stop him, calm him down. But he just lost it. He grabbed a broken bottle and..." her voice caught in her throat. "He stabbed her in the eye."

The words hung in the air between them, heavy and horrifying. Ella could still see the blood, Peg's screams of terror echoing in her mind.

"She lost the eye. The doctors couldn't save it. They did everything they could, but..." she trailed off, shaking her head.

"And Todd..." Ella's voice hardened slightly after a period of silence. "He just ran away, disappearing for weeks. When he finally returned, he acted like nothing happened, like it was all just a big misunderstanding."

Dory remained silent, her brow furrowed in deep contemplation. When she finally spoke, her voice was heavy with sympathy and determination. "What happened to the guy Peg was seeing?"

Ella's gaze dropped to her feet. "After her disfigurement, it wasn't long before the relationship ended. He couldn't handle it, I guess. Just another disappointment in Peg's life."

Dory nodded cautiously. The puzzle pieces were shifting, forming a new and troubling picture. "So, you think Todd might be involved somehow with Oscar's death?"

Ella shrugged, her eyes flicking away from Dory's penetrating gaze. "I didn't before, but now I can't say." Her voice grew hesitant. "Todd has a history of violence and a complicated relationship with me and Oscar. It's hard to imagine, but I can't ignore the possibility anymore."

Chapter 13

Dory knocked on Todd's door, mind still reeling from her previous discoveries. When he opened it, she noticed the flicker of surprise in his eyes. He immediately masked it with a neutral expression.

"Detective Dingess," he greeted, stepping aside to let her in. His voice carried a hint of wariness, barely perceptible beneath his polite tone. "What brings you here?"

Dory stepped into the apartment, scanning over the cluttered room. Random collectibles and music memorabilia covered practically every living space. "I wanted to talk to you about Ella's diary," she spoke seriously. "Why did you give it to me?"

Todd shrugged, his eyes averted as if afraid to meet the detective's gaze. "I thought it might be helpful in the investigation. Ella and Oscar were close, but they had their problems, too. I thought it might shed some light on their relationship."

She nodded and took a seat on the couch, voice carefully neutral. "I read through the entries. Ella had a lot of resentment towards Oscar." She watched Todd closely for any reaction. "But there's something else I wanted to ask you about."

Todd's posture stiffened. "What's that?"

Dory leaned forward, her elbows resting on her knees as she fixed Todd with a firm gaze. "Were you in love with Ella when she was male?"

He nodded slowly, surprise in his voice. "I was young. I never had a crush on a boy before; he was my stepbrother at the time. It was confusing."

Todd sighed and ran a shaky hand through his hair. "Look, I won't deny that my feelings for Ella were... complex," he admitted hesitantly. "But that was a long time ago. When she transitioned, things changed between us. I saw her as a sister, nothing more."

Dory's look was thoughtful, taking in every word and analyzing it. She leaned back slightly, her posture relaxing a fraction. "And Oscar?"

"Oscar was different," he said wistfully, eyes filled with deep longing. "He was kind and gentle, with a heart big enough to love everyone. When we started dating, it felt right. Like we were meant to be together, you know?"

"I understand," she nodded slowly, her voice hinting warmth. "But I need to know the truth, Todd. Did you have anything to do with his death?"

His face grew contorted with grief as if the idea was a physical blow. "No," he cried out. "I would never hurt Oscar! I loved him. I still do. He was everything to me! How could you even think that?"

"I must follow every lead in this investigation, and you're a person of interest right now. It's my job to consider all possibilities, no matter how painful they may be."

Dory relaxed her shoulders. "There's something else I need to ask you about, Todd." She sighed, but her voice remained measured. "We received a tip that Oscar may have been involved with drugs or a drug dealer. It's a lead we can't ignore."

"Drugs?" Todd repeated, his brow tightened. "No, that's impossible. Oscar wasn't into that scene at all."

"Are you sure about that?" Dory probed, her tone insistent. "Sometimes people can hide these things, even from those closest to them. It's not uncommon in cases like this."

Todd shook his head vehemently. "No, you wouldn't understand. Oscar was adamantly against drugs. He saw what they did to some of our friends in the music scene. He wouldn't even touch the stuff."

"But you went to gigs together, didn't you?" Dory pressed. "Surely you've seen drugs being passed around?"

Todd ran a hand through his hair. "Of course. It was everywhere if you knew where to look. But Oscar always stayed away. He'd have a beer or two, but that was it. He was always the responsible one."

She studied his face intently, searching for deception. "What about you, Todd? Have you ever been involved with drugs?"

Todd's jaw clenched, a flicker of something—shame, perhaps—crossing his features before he answered. "I experimented a little in college," he admitted reluctantly. "But I've been clean for years. Oscar was a big part of why I stopped. He supported me through it all, never judged me."

Dory's eyes narrowed as she spoke. "There's something else I need to ask you," she paused, leaning closer. "What happened to Peg's eye? More importantly, what was your involvement?"

Todd flinched as if he had been struck. For a long moment, he said nothing, his jaw working as if he were chewing on the words, trying to force them out.

"It was an accident," he rushed out. "We were arguing, and things got... out of hand."

"What were you arguing about? I need details, Todd."

His eyes shot away, face flushing with shame. "My mother... she was seeing someone. A man. I disapproved of." He swallowed hard.

"You need to tell me everything, Todd. This is an official investigation; any information you withhold could be considered obstruction of justice." Dingess paused, allowing her words to sink in. "Start from the beginning. What happened that day?"

Todd's eyes squeezed shut, his face contorting with the pain of remembrance. "I lashed out. I was just so angry, so hurt. But I swear I didn't mean it."

He took a ragged breath, chest heaving with the effort. "I had broken a bottle earlier. It was just there, sitting on the counter. I grabbed it without thinking, and then... then it was over. It happened so fast."

The detective's pen froze on the page mid-sentence. "You stabbed your mother?"

His head jerked up abruptly, his eyes wild with panic and desperation. "No! No, I didn't... I would never do that intentionally!" he exclaimed. "You have to believe me!"

Todd buried his face in his trembling hands, his shoulders shaking with his sobs. "The bottle... it slipped from my grasp," he continued brokenly. "I was just trying to get her to listen, to understand. But then suddenly there was blood everywhere, and she was screaming, and I didn't know what to do. It all happened so fast."

"Todd, I know this is hard. But you have to tell me everything. What happened next?"

Todd's shoulders slumped. "I panicked," he admitted, rubbing his eyes. "I called 911, and then I ran. I was so scared, so ashamed. I couldn't face what I'd done."

He finally looked up at the detective, his eyes shimmering with tears. "I never meant to hurt her. I swear I never meant for any of it to happen."

Dory nodded, taking in the gravity of his confession. "Thank you for being honest, Todd. I appreciate your cooperation."

She stood up slowly, gathering her notes. "I'll need you to come down to the station to make an official statement about the incident with Peg. And as for Oscar's case, we'll contact you if we need further information."

"I understand. I'll do whatever I can to help."

Todd eventually led her to the apartment door, a polite but anxious smile on his lips as the door shut with a click.

As the detective walked down the barren hallways, she mulled the story over in her head. Todd's story was tragic, and his remorse seemed genuine. Still, she knew she couldn't let empathy cloud her judgment. She had a job to do, and she was determined to uncover the truth about Oscar's death, no matter where it led.

Chapter 14

Dory entered the crowded coffeehouse, scanning the room until her eyes locked with Peg's. She was busy serving customers, and her usual friendly demeanor was apparent. Peg flashed her a warm, welcoming smile, gesturing with a tilt of her head for Dory to take a seat at the counter.

She finished up with a customer and made her way over to Dory, who had slid onto a worn leather stool. Peg adjusted her ruffled apron, evidence of a busy morning. "Detective Dingess," she greeted warmly. "What can I get for you today?"

"Actually, Peg, I was hoping we could talk," Dory sighed, her tone carrying a subtle weight. "I just came from speaking with Todd."

Her smile wavered briefly, a flicker of concern crossing in her good eye. She quickly regained her composure. "Of course, Detective. Just give me a moment."

Peg turned to Ella, who was busy wiping down countertops. "Ella, honey, could you keep an eye on things out here for a while? I need to speak with the detective in the back."

Ella straightened up, tucking a stray strand of hair behind her ear. She nodded reassuringly. "Sure thing, Peg. I've got it covered."

Peg wore a grateful smile before turning back to Dory. "Follow me, Detective. We can talk in the office."

Peg led the way through the coffeehouse, navigating through a maze of tables and chairs with familiarity. Towards the back, they stepped through a large, windowed door. *Employees Only* was written across the front in bold, cursive letters.

Once settled into the office, Peg leaned against the worn wooden desk. Her arms crossed over her chest, a defensive posture that didn't escape Dory's keen eye. "So, what did Todd have to say?"

"He told me about your eye," she began, her tone gentle yet direct. "About how it happened."

Peg's hand instinctively went to cover her left eye, shielding it from view. It was a guarded habit Dory observed, a telltale sign of the deep-seated trauma that she had to endure.

"I see," Peg said, unreadable. "And what exactly did he tell you?"

"He said it was an accident, that he was drunk and angry and lashed out. That he threw a bottle, and it shattered, and a piece of glass hit you in the eye."

Peg remained silent for a long moment. Finally, she sighed. "It wasn't an accident." Her words felt heavy with the weight of long-held secrets. "He was aiming at me. He wanted to hurt me."

Dory nodded in understanding, a look of empathy crossing her features. "I'm so sorry, Peg. No one should have to go through something like that."

"It's in the past now. I've learned to live with it. To adapt," Peg said, her voice growing stronger as she spoke. She absently fidgeted with her apron, eyes glued to the floor. "You'd be surprised what a person can get used to, given enough time."

There was a slight shift in Dory's demeanor as she prepared to broach another sensitive topic. "There's something else I need to ask you about, Peg. Your relationship with Mitch."

Her body visibly stiffened, and she gripped the edge of the desk. "What about it?" she asked her voice tight with hardly concealed anxiety.

"I know that you and Mitch had a... complicated history," Dory swallowed. "That your relationship began while he was still married to Adelaide?"

She took a slow, deliberate breath before answering. "Yes, that's true," she admitted, her voice carrying regret. "Mitch and I... we fell in love. It wasn't something either of us planned, but it happened."

"And how did Adelaide react when she found out?" Dory pressed gently.

Peg laughed, a harsh sound that echoed through the room. "How do you think she reacted? She was furious, of course. She felt I had stolen her husband, her family, her entire life."

"And did you? Did you steal her family?"

"No, I didn't. Mitch and Adelaide's marriage was already falling apart when he and I got together. It was a mess long before I came into the picture. I didn't cause their problems, Detective. I was just caught in the middle of a crumbling relationship."

Dory wrote a few things into her notepad, and her pen eventually slowed and froze on the page. She glanced up. "Peg, I need to ask you about Mitch's death. Can you tell me what happened?"

Peg's expression darkened, and she looked away, her voice coming out strained. "It was a hit-and-run. Mitch was walking home from a night with his friends at O'Malley's, the bar down the street. He was crossing the road when a car came out of nowhere and hit him. The driver never stopped, never even slowed down."

Dory nodded, her pen hovering over her notepad. "And this was about ten years ago, right?"

Peg nodded, a sad look on her face. "Yes. It was devastating for all of us. Mitch was the glue that held our family together. Without him, everything just... fell apart.

"I'm so sorry for your loss, Peg. I can't imagine how hard it must have been."

Peg took a shaky breath and wiped her eye with the back of her hand. "It was. But we had to move on, you know?"

Dory leaned forward, still sympathetic. "Do you think there was anything suspicious about Mitch's accident? Anything that might indicate it wasn't a random hit-and-run?"

"I don't know. I've thought about it, of course. If someone had a reason to want to hurt Mitch, I could never come up with anything concrete."

Dory made another note, her expression unreadable. "And what about the aftermath? Was there a life insurance payout?"

Peg nodded, her shoulders slumping. "Yes, there was. A decent sum, actually."

"And who inherited that?"

Peg took a deep breath, her hands clenched in her lap. "The coffeehouse went to me, as did a portion of Mitch's other assets. He had a will and left almost everything to me. Oscar and Ella were taken care of, too. There were trusts set up for both of them, with a significant amount. It was meant to help with their education and future."

"And Adelaide? Did she inherit anything from Mitch?" Dingess asked, searching for a reaction.

Peg shook her head, a hint of discomfort crossing her features. "No, she didn't. Mitch changed his will a couple of months before he died. Adelaide was cut out completely."

"How did Adelaide react to that?" Dory's pen remained poised over her notepad.

"She was furious, of course. Livid. She felt she had been cheated out of what was rightfully hers. There were some ugly confrontations after the will was read." Peg sighed defeatedly. "It only made things more complicated between all of us."

Dory studied Peg for a long moment, sensing the weight of the memories pressing down on her. "I appreciate you being so open with me, Peg. I know digging up the past like this can't be easy."

Peg waved her hand dismissively, but her expression told a different story. "It's okay, Detective. Whatever I can do to help you find answers about Oscar."

A brief period of silence overtook them. "Can you tell me more about the relationship you had after Mitch died?" Dory finally asked. "The one that Todd didn't approve of—the fight that led to your eye injury."

"His name was Jack. Jack Carlson," she breathed. "He was a regular at the coffeehouse and came in most mornings for his usual black coffee and a blueberry scone. He always sat by the window, reading his newspaper."

Dory nodded encouragingly. "And how did your relationship with Jack begin?"

Peg shrugged, a wistful smile tugging at the corners of her mouth. "It was about a year and a half after Mitch died. I was struggling, trying to keep the coffeehouse afloat and attempting to deal with my grief at the same time. Jack was kind to me and always had a smile and a kind word. He'd stay a little longer each day, and we'd talk. One day, out of the blue, he asked me out to dinner. And I... Well, I said yes."

"How did Todd react when he learned about your relationship with Jack?"

Peg's face darkened, and she forced herself to look away. "Oh, he was furious," she said, her voice thick with emotion. "He said I was betraying Mitch's memory, that I had no right to be seeing someone so soon after his death. The words cut deep, you know? I was still grieving, too, but I was trying to move forward."

"And that's when the fight happened?"

"Yes. Todd was drunk and angrier than I'd ever seen him. He started throwing things and yelling at me. I tried to calm him down and reason with him, but he wouldn't listen. And then, before I knew it, he had a broken bottle in his hand..."

"I'm so sorry, Peg. That must have been a terrible experience for you."

"It was," she said, her voice rough. She swallowed hard before continuing. "But something even worse happened afterward. Jack came to the hospital to see me a few times, but he couldn't handle all the drama. Maybe he couldn't be with someone who looked like me, either. At least, that's what I think."

Silence fell in the room. Peg ran a hand through her hair before speaking again. Her expression softened. "I can't say I blame him for getting out while he could. It was a lot to take on, especially for a new relationship."

Dory leaned back in the chair, pensive. She tapped her pen lightly against the notepad. "And what about Todd? Your relationship with him changed after the incident, right?"

"It's changed," Peg admitted, her voice heavy with regret. "I've forgiven him, but every so often, when I look in the mirror, I'm reminded of what he did to me."

Dory gave a look of understanding. "Peg, there is something else I need to ask. Something that might be hard to talk about."

"What is it, Detective?" she asked apprehensively, her one good eye trained on the detective's face.

Dory chose her words carefully. "I know that Oscar and Todd were both musicians. They played in a band together. I was wondering... do you know if they were into drugs at all? Or... if their bandmates or anyone at the recording studio might have been involved with that scene?"

Peg's eyes widened, and for a moment, it looked like she might not answer. "I had my suspicions," she finally admitted, her voice low and troubled. "I knew the music scene could be pretty wild. I was worried about the kind of people my kids could be hanging out with. You hear stories, you know?"

"Did you ever see any signs of drug use? Or hear anyone talk about it?"

Peg's brow furrowed. "Not directly, no. But sometimes Oscar and Todd would come home late at night and be... different. Jittery, almost. Like they were on edge."

"And what about their bandmates?" Dory asked, making a small gesture with her hand. "Did you ever meet any of them? Notice anything unusual?"

"A few times, yeah. They seemed like decent guys, but you never know what people are like behind closed doors."

"I have reason to believe that Oscar may have been involved with a local drug dealer. That he was in some trouble," Dory said, watching Peg's reaction closely.

The revelation seemed to catch her off guard, and a flicker of disbelief crossed her face. Peg sighed, her one good eye searching the room as if the answers might be hidden in the corners.

"Tell me right now what you're hiding from me, Peg," Dory pressed, her gaze intense.

Peg brushed a graying hair from her face. "I'm sorry, Detective," she said, feeble. "I wish I could tell you more, but Oscar was so secretive about the whole thing. He came to me one night, desperate and scared, and begged me for money."

She paused, swallowing hard before continuing, "I've never seen him like that before. It scared me, Detective. It scared me more than I can say."

Dory leaned in closer, her pen frozen on the notepad. "And what happened next, Peg?"

Peg breathed, hands twisting in her lap as if she were trying to wring out the painful memories. "I gave him the money," she eventually confessed. "I didn't want to, but I was so afraid for him. I thought if I could help him this one time, he'd be okay. That it would be enough to get him out of whatever mess he'd gotten himself into."

"And did he pay off the dealer?" Dingess probed.

"He said he did," Peg replied, her good eye searching the Detective's face. "He promised me it was over, that he'd never get involved with anything like that again."

"And did you believe him?"

Peg was silent for a moment. "I wanted to," she said, words heavy with regret. "God knows, I wanted to. But part of me always wondered and worried if he was okay."

"And you never told anyone?" Dory pressed. "Not even Adelaide or Ella?"

"No, I couldn't. I promised Oscar that I'd keep it a secret. And after he went missing, I just... I couldn't stand the thought of people knowing. That they would think less of him."

"I understand, Peg," Dory said softly, her pen scratching across the paper. "But this information could be crucial for the investigation. How long ago was this?"

Peg's shoulders sagged, the weight of her long-held secret visibly lifting. She sifted through the months in her mind. "About nine months ago."

Dory nodded, jotting down the timeline. "Is there anything else you can tell me? Anything about the dealer or the circumstances of Oscar's debt?"

Peg's brow furrowed as she strained to remember. "I don't know anything else, Detective. Oscar didn't tell me much, and I didn't ask. I just wanted it to be over and for him to be safe. Maybe it was selfish of me not to push harder."

"If you can think of anything else, anything at all that might be relevant... it could be essential to the investigation," Dory urged, leaning forward slightly.

Peg nodded, her shoulders sagging as she wiped away the fallen tears. The weight of her secret, which she finally shared, seemed to have both unburdened and exhausted her.

Dory stood, her hand outstretched. "Thank you, Peg. I know this hasn't been easy for you. If you can think of anything else, please call me."

Chapter 15

Ella clocked out and stepped into the cool evening air, the bell above the coffeehouse's door chiming a last farewell. The streets were lit dimly by warm, flickering streetlights. Unease crept over her. She pulled her jacket tighter around her body as she walked, trying to ward off the cold and the growing feeling that someone was watching her.

Her footsteps echoed onto the pavement. She quickened her pace, eager to get home.

Behind her, there was a soft thud. Ella's grip tightened on the strap of her bag as she cast a furtive glance over her shoulder, scanning the darkened storefronts and alleyways for any sign of movement. She tried to chalk it up to nothing.

The wind whistled through the trees lining the sidewalk, and the rustling leaves sounded like whispers as if the city itself was trying to warn her of lurking doom. She glanced over her shoulder every few steps, brown hair whipping around her face, but the streets behind her were empty.

Could it be Oscar's ghost haunting her? Could it be the homeless man's murderer stalking the streets for their next victim?

Ella shook her head, trying to dismiss the thought. She was letting her fear get the better of her, conjuring up ghosts and bogeymen in the shadows. Still, she couldn't shake the feeling that something was different that night.

As she turned the corner onto her street, Ella caught sight of a shadowy figure emerging from an alleyway ahead of her. Her heart leaped into her throat, and without a second thought, she started to run, her bag slamming against her side with every frantic step.

She didn't dare look back; her mind focused solely on reaching the safety of her building. She fumbled with her keys, her hands shaking violently as she struggled to unlock the door.

Finally, it swung open with a creak. Relief washed over her as she burst through the front door of the building. Bracing against the wall, she held a hand over her heaving chest, trying to catch her breath. *This is foolish*, she thought, *like a child afraid of the dark.*

But the unease persisted.

The ancient elevator groaned as it carried Ella to the seventh floor, the rusted cables straining with every floor they passed. She pressed herself into the corner, eyes tightly shut, avoiding touching the grimy walls. She couldn't wait to get out of this place—the peeling wallpaper, the dim flickering light bulbs that cast eerie shadows, the pervasive smell of decay that seeped through every crevice.

As the elevator stuttered to a halt, she smoothed her hands over her jacket and took a steadying breath. Maybe she had just been letting her nerves get the better of her on the walk home. She was safe now, away from the looming darkness on the street.

But when the elevator doors squealed open, her relief was short-lived. Muffled shouts filtered through the closed door of her apartment down the dingy hall. She entered the apartment, the muffled sounds of a heated argument between Adelaide and Frank drifting from the bedroom. Their voices, though indistinct, carried tension.

Ella paused with her hand on the doorknob, straining to hear the words. She could hear Frank's deep, agitated tone, followed by her mother's retorts. The walls seemed to vibrate with the intensity of their disagreement—a familiar knot of anxiety formed in her stomach.

Cautiously, she moved toward the kitchen; her footsteps light on the creaking floorboards as she tried to distance herself. But the voices only seemed to grow louder and more insistent. Her mind raced, wondering what could have sparked such a volatile confrontation.

Snippets of the argument reached her ears, fragmented and unclear. "Can't go on like this..." Frank's usually calm voice came out strained. Adelaide's response was clipped and harsh.

Her mother's relationship with Frank had been strained. Oscar's death and the ensuing investigation had taken a toll, adding some tension to their interactions. But never like this.

Ella leaned against the counter, sipping water and trying to block out the muffled voices. Her stomach twisted into a leaden knot as she detected Frank's lower timbre, attempting to respond, though she couldn't quite make out his words. She moved cautiously down the hall, straining to listen through the thin walls.

She pressed herself nearly flat against the wall, straining to make out the words filtering through. Her heart pounded in her ears.

"Don't try to blame this whole thing on me!" Frank's voice rose, sharp with accusation. "You're the one who argued with Oscar that night. You were the one who made him leave the apartment in a rage."

Frank's accusation hung heavy in the bedroom, his words cutting through the tense silence. Adelaide stared at him, eyes wide with shock and disbelief. She stepped backward quickly, steadying herself against the dresser.

"You couldn't accept his relationship with Todd," Frank continued. "You couldn't stand the thought of your son being with his stepbrother!"

"What are you talking about?" she asked shakily. "No, that's not true. We had a disagreement, but I never wanted anything to happen to him."

Frank sighed, his shoulders sagging. "Adelaide, I know what happened that night. I heard the argument, the shouting. I saw Oscar run out of the apartment, and then..."

He trailed off, unable to finish the sentence. Adelaide shook her head, her mind reeling as she tried to process Frank's words. "No, no, that's not possible. Oscar, he couldn't have fallen. He was upset, but he wouldn't have been so reckless."

Ella felt her knees buckle beneath her. She slid down the wall, her body shaking with silent sobs. The image of her brother falling to his death played over and over in her mind.

Frank took a step closer, his eyes searching Adelaide's face. His voice grew softer. "Adelaide, I saw the elevator doors open. I heard his body hitting the bottom of the shaft. I know what happened."

Adelaide sank onto the bed, her head in her hands. "Oh God, what have I done?" she whispered, choked with emotion. "I was so angry, so upset about him and Todd. I never meant for this to happen."

Frank knelt beside her, his hand resting gently on her shoulder. "I know you didn't mean for it to happen, Adelaide. But it did. And I couldn't let you take the blame. You just had too much to drink that night."

Adelaide looked up at him, eyes brimmed with tears. "You covered it up? You lied for me?"

Frank nodded, his expression somber. "I did what I had to do, Adelaide. I care about you deeply, and I couldn't bear to see you punished for something that wasn't your fault."

The room fell silent, and Ella could hear nothing but her heartbeat in her ears. The truth about Oscar's death had finally been revealed, and it was too much to bear.

Adelaide's tears spilled over, and she buried her face in Frank's chest, her body shaking with sobs. Frank held her close.

"What are you saying, Frank?" Adelaide pulled away. "You... you moved Oscar's body? You covered up his death?"

Frank nodded, his expression somber. "I did what I had to do. I moved his body to protect you. I couldn't let you take the blame for something that was an accident."

A raw, anguished wail clawed its way from Adelaide's depths, reverberating like the howl of a wounded animal.

Adelaide shook her head vehemently. "But it wasn't my fault, Frank. It was an accident. How could you keep this from me for so long?"

Ella remained frozen outside the door, her lungs burning as she denied herself even the shallowest breaths.

"Frank, the elevator..." Adelaide's voice trembled with anger. "It was your responsibility to keep it maintained! If you had done your job properly, this wouldn't have happened. Oscar would still be alive."

Frank looked away, unable to meet her eyes. "I never meant for this to happen, Adelaide. I'd do anything to protect you."

Adelaide shot up. "Protect me? By lying? By covering up the death of my son?" Her eyes narrowed as a terrible thought occurred to her. "And what about the homeless man, Frank? Did you do something to him to keep him quiet?"

Frank's prolonged silence was the only answer she needed. A choked sob escaped her lips. "Oh God, Frank..." Horror dawned in her eyes. "What have you done?"

Frank reached out, delicate as he tried to touch her arm. "Adelaide, please," he pleaded. "I did it for you. I did it for us."

Ella leaned closer to the door, her breath caught in her throat as she waited to hear Frank's next words.

"I think he saw me move Oscar's body that night. I didn't know what to do and couldn't risk him telling anyone what he saw. I had to do something. I couldn't let him ruin everything; I couldn't let him destroy our lives. I had to protect you, to protect us."

Adelaide jerked away, her eyes blazing with fury. "No, Frank. You did it for yourself. You're a murderer!"

Ella felt the blood drain from her face. She clasped a hand over her mouth, stifling the whimpers in her constricted throat. A nightmarish reality took shape—her brother was dead, and her mother and Frank were responsible.

The sound of footsteps approaching the door jolted Ella out of her trance. She scrambled to her feet, wiping the tears that flowed freely down her cheeks. She couldn't let them find her here, couldn't let them see the pain and betrayal etched across her features.

She stumbled down the hallway, vision blurred by tears. The weight of truth crashed down upon her. From the corner of her eye, she could see that the door to the apartment was ajar, a sliver of light spilling in from the hallway.

She called for Iris in a hushed tone, her voice barely a whisper, but there was no familiar jingling of a collar or soft meow in response.

Panic rose in her chest as she quickly and silently searched each room, her movements frantic yet controlled. She looked under the bed, peering into the shadowy recesses. She threw clothes aside and checked the closet, hoping to find Iris curled up in a cozy nook.

Inhaling deeply to calm her nerves, Ella headed into the hallway to search the building. Her fingers were weak as she pulled the door closed behind her, the familiar creak of the hinges echoing in the empty corridor. She paused, straining her ears for any sound revealing where Iris could be.

Inside the apartment, the tension between Adelaide and Frank reached a fever pitch. Adelaide's eyes darted around the room, hands shaking as she tried to process what Frank had revealed.

Fearing that Ella would be home soon, she reached for her phone but, with trembling fingers, had trouble unlocking the screen.

"What are you doing?" Frank demanded, his voice low and menacing. He took a step toward her, eyes narrowed into slits.

"I need to check my texts! Ella usually texts me on her way home. She should know what she's walking into." Her fingers hovered over the screen, desperately trying to input the correct passcode.

Frank's eyes narrowed, a flicker of panic crossing his face. He lunged forward, closing his hand on Adelaide's wrist in a vice-like grip. "No. You're not going to text anyone," he growled, his face inches from hers. "I won't let you ruin everything, not after everything I've done for you."

"Don't put your hands on me!" Adelaide cried, struggling against his grip, her eyes blazing with anger and desperation. She knew he would stop at nothing to keep his secrets safe. She twisted her arm to break free, but Frank's grip only tightened.

Frank's expression hardened, and an icy determination settled over his features. The lines around his eyes deepened, giving him a haunted look. He exhaled a sharp breath. "I'm sorry, Adelaide. But I can't let you do this." His voice was eerily calm, starkly contrasting to the violence beneath the surface.

Adelaide managed to yank herself away with a pitched scream.

Frank reached out, his hand closing around the base of a heavy lamp on the dresser. In one swift motion, he brought it down onto Adelaide's head before she could run, the sickening crunch of metal against bone filling the room.

Adelaide crumpled to the floor immediately, her phone clattering from her hand and skidding across the hardwood. Frank towered over her, his chest heaving with exertion. He stared down at her motionless form. He had to act quickly before Ella returned and discovered what he'd done.

He snatched Adelaide's phone from the floor, thick fingers trembling as he attempted to unlock it. He cursed under his breath as he punched in the numbers that he thought he knew by heart. Adelaide had changed the passcode.

He'd find another way to stop Ella from learning the truth.

Chapter 16

Dory sat at her desk, eyes glued to the glowing screen of her phone. The precinct was quiet at that hour, the only sound being the low hum of fluorescent lights overhead. She had spent hours poring over the case files, trying to piece together clues that would lead her to the truth about Oscar's death.

Suddenly, her phone buzzed with an incoming message. She saw Adelaide's name flash across the top of the screen. She opened the text with curiosity, her eyes widening as she read the fragmented message: *Find Ella it's Fra—*

A sense of dread washed over her. She knew instinctively that something was wrong, that Adelaide and Ella were in danger. Without hesitation, she grabbed her coat and rushed out of the precinct, her mind racing with worst-case scenarios.

She dialed Ella's number as she hurried to her car, but the call went straight to voicemail. Dory cursed under her breath.

She peeled out of the parking lot, tires screeching against the asphalt. As she navigated the busy streets of Bay Ridge, weaving through traffic with practiced precision, her mind grew consumed with increasingly dire scenarios. What if something already happened? What if she was too late?

She forcefully put those thoughts aside, focusing on the urgent task at hand. She had to get to the apartment and ensure Ella and Adelaide were safe.

Dory hit a red light, her foot tapping impatiently on the accelerator. Every second counted, and the delay felt like an eternity. She gripped the steering wheel tightly, knuckles white with tension.

She was acutely aware that she was in her vehicle without the benefit of lights or sirens to clear her path. The traffic around her continued to move at its leisurely pace, oblivious to her urgency.

She reached for her radio, quickly switching it on. "Roll additional units to 380 Ridge Blvd, Unit 7C. Potential 10-32, Capitol-One in progress, requesting immediate backup. I'm en route in an unmarked vehicle." Her words were clipped and urgent.

The dispatcher's voice crackled back, confirming the request. The moment the light turned green, she gunned the engine, weaving through the cars ahead of her with reckless determination.

When she finally reached the apartment building, she jumped out of the car before it had fully stopped, leaving the driver's door wide open. She ran to the entrance, her eyes scanning the darkened windows for movement, instinctively reaching for the weapon at her hip.

The night air was cold and damp, and she could see her breath forming clouds before her face. The streetlights cast shadows across the crumbling facade of the building, making it look even more foreboding than usual.

She entered with her senses on high alert. She could hear the floorboards creaking beneath her feet as she approached the stairs. Despite being in the building countless times, something about it felt different that night—the hairs on the back of her neck stood at attention, unable to shake the feeling that danger lurked around every corner.

Meanwhile, Ella descended the narrow steps, her footsteps echoing off the concrete walls. The air grew colder with each step, and the murky smell of the basement made her cough. She strained her eyes in the dim light.

"Iris!" she called out breathily, her voice bouncing off the damp walls. "Where are you, baby? Please come out."

She descended the stairs, trying to quell the feeling that something was very wrong. The air was thick and oppressive, and shadows seemed to linger with every passing moment. Every creak and groan sent a shiver through her.

Unbeknownst to Ella, her cries for the cat had not gone unnoticed. Frank, hidden in the shadows, watched her every move.

A sinister grin spread across his face as he realized the opportunity that had presented itself. He stepped out from behind a stack of boxes, footsteps heavy and deliberate. The sound of his movement was nearly masked by the constant drip of water from a nearby leaky pipe.

Ella gasped as his footsteps drew nearer. She backed away, hands fumbling behind her, searching for anything she could use to defend herself.

"Frank, what are you doing?"

Frank didn't respond; his face twisted into a menacing snarl. He advanced quickly like a predator among its prey. His eyes, usually unremarkable, now gleamed with a sinister look.

Ella's fingers closed around a rusted pipe lying on the ground, and she gripped it tightly, thrusting it out in front of her like a weapon. "Stay back!"

A sudden meow cut through the tension, startling the both of them. Quickly, Ella's gaze darted to the corner of the basement, where a pair of glowing eyes stared back at her.

"Iris!" she cried, momentary relief flooding through her.

The cat emerged from the shadows, her tail twitching back and forth. She seemed unperturbed by Frank's menacing presence, focusing solely on Ella.

Seizing the opportunity, Ella swiftly scooped Iris up and clutched her tightly to her chest. She backed away immediately, keeping her makeshift weapon pointed at Frank.

"Don't do anything stupid, Frank," she warned, her eyes narrowing as she summoned every ounce of courage.

Frank paused, his eyes darting between Ella and the pipe in her hand. A tense silence hung in the air, thick with unspoken threats.

Finally, Frank stepped back, his hands raised in mock surrender. "Fine," he growled. "Have it your way." His eyes narrowed, a silent promise that this wasn't over.

Ella didn't wait for him to change his mind. She turned and raced up the stairs, lungs burning with exertion. Iris clung to her t-shirt with sharp claws.

She spotted the elevator doors cracked just ahead as she reached the main floor. Without hesitation, she dove in, slamming her hand against the button to close them.

The elevator lurched into motion. Ella breathed a sigh of relief—she had escaped Frank, at least for now.

She leaned against the wall of the elevator, legs shaky. Iris meowed softly in her grasp, likely sensing the distress radiating from her. Ella stroked the cat's fur, attempting to calm her own racing heart.

But as the elevator climbed, a sudden jolt violently rocked the car, throwing Ella off balance. She quickly gripped the handlebar behind her, pulling Iris tight against her chest.

Her stomach dropped as the elevator ground to a halt with an ear-splitting screech, the cables groaning in protest. The following silence was deafening, broken only by Ella's ragged breaths and Iris's distressed mewling.

She was trapped.

Detective Dingess was halfway up the stairs when she heard the commotion. The sound of metal screeching against metal echoed through the building, followed by a chilling silence. Her heart skipped a beat as she realized where the noise was coming from.

She raced towards the elevator, her feet pounding against the steps. As she approached, the lights in the hallway flickered ominously before plunging the area into darkness. Her blood ran cold. Every second counted.

Suddenly, a wail pierced the silence, echoing through the stairwell like a gunshot. Dory's heart stopped. She knew that scream. It was Ella, and she was in trouble.

Chapter 17

The lights inside the elevator eventually flickered back to life, casting an unsteady glow across the confined space. The car lurched upward again with a series of unsettling creaks and groans. Ella thought of Oscar's last moments. A wave of nausea washed over her, a sickening sense of déjà vu taking hold.

The elevator jolted violently again, coming to an abrupt halt between floors, sending Ella stumbling against the wall. She screamed in pain as her shoulder collided with the hard metal surface. Iris yowled in terror and leaped from her arms.

The lights cast eerie shadows across the small space. Ella's heart pounded in her ears as she watched the numbers above the door flicker and die, leaving her in suffocating darkness.

Her breath came in short, ragged gasps. The walls seemed to close around her. Tears stung her eyes as she whispered a silent prayer, pleading for a miracle to spare her from the same terrifying end.

"Help!" she screamed, her voice raw with fear. "Somebody help me!" Her cries echoed in the small space, amplifying her terror.

But there was no response, no sound of anyone coming to her aid. Tears continued to stream down her face as she hugged Iris tighter.

"Oscar," she whispered, her voice shaky. "If you can hear me, please help me. I need you now more than ever."

She closed her eyes, and for a moment, she swore she could feel Oscar's presence as if he were right there with her in the elevator. The sensation was so intense that she almost reached out to touch him.

"Please forgive me," she pleaded. "I'm so sorry for everything. For not being there, for not understanding. I'd give anything to make it right."

The elevator lurched again, the cables groaning in protest. Ella flinched, her eyes flying open as she returned to the present.

She stared at the spasming lights, shadows dancing across the walls. Each flicker seemed to taunt her, reminding her of her precarious situation and genuine danger.

"We have to get out of here," she trembled out, clutching Iris tighter.

Ella took a deep breath, steeling her nerves. She sat Iris down and rose to her feet, eyes scanning the cramped space for a way out. The elevator felt smaller than ever.

Dory approached and heard more commotion from the elevator. Her heart raced as she realized Ella was in danger. Without hesitation, Dory rushed closer, up the stairs and to the closest vantage point.

"Ella!" she cried out, her voice echoing through the stairwell. "Hang on, I'm coming! Just stay calm!"

Dingess, Ella thought to herself, a breath of slight relief escaping her. She pounded on the elevator's inner walls.

Dory reached the seventh floor, her footsteps thundering on the concrete stairs as she neared Ella's cries. But just as she approached, the entire building was plunged into darkness. Quickly, she fumbled for her flashlight, her hands shaking as she clicked it on. The beam cut through the blackness and illuminated the worn metal of the elevator doors.

"Ella, can you hear me?" she called out urgently. Dory pressed her ear against the cold metal doors, feeling the chill seep into her skin. She strained to hear any sound from within, and her breath caught in her throat.

From inside the elevator, Ella's muffled sobs reached Dory's ears. "Yes! Help me, please!" Ella pleaded, her voice filled with terror. "I don't want to die!"

"Okay, Ella, I need you to listen to me," Dory said, her voice calm and reassuring despite the panic threatening to overwhelm her. "I'm going to get you out of there, but I need you to stay calm, alright?"

She reached for her radio, her voice steady but urgent as she spoke: "This is Detective Dingess. We need the fire department at 380 Ridge Blvd immediately. We have a civilian trapped in an elevator due to mechanical failure. The situation is critical."

Dory turned her attention to the control panel, fingers dancing over the buttons as she tried to override the system. Sweat beaded on her forehead as she punched in various combinations. But the elevator remained stubbornly still, trapped between floors, its mechanisms making unpleasant and worrying noises.

Just then, the elevator gave another loud shudder, the metal screeching against metal as it lurched downward in the shaft.

Ella screamed.

She was falling.

"If you can hear me, Oscar, please help me!"

Chapter 18

Adelaide opened her eyes, a dull throb pulsing through her skull as she slowly regained consciousness. She pushed herself up, wincing at the excruciating pain that pierced her throbbing head like sharpened blades. She blinked, trying to clear her vision, but the room spun around her. Disoriented, she took a moment to get her bearings, the memories of her confrontation with Frank flooding back in fragmented pieces.

Panic gripped her as she realized the full gravity of the situation. She staggered to her feet, swaying unsteadily as the room spun around her. With trembling limbs, she stumbled toward the door, gripping it with one bloody hand. A single thought consumed her mind: she had to find Ella before it was too late.

As she stepped out into the dark hallway, Dory's prominent voice reached her ears, echoing from somewhere nearby. Adelaide followed the sound, her heart hammering in her chest.

She heard a commotion from the direction of the elevator shaft. Muffled voices rang out, their direction now imperceptible. Adelaide's breath caught in her throat as she recognized the familiar tones—it was Dory and Ella, and they were frantic.

"Ella! Dory!" Adelaide cried, her voice hoarse with fear.

She moved toward the elevator, her steps uneven and faltering. She could hear Dory's voice more clearly now, but it sounded like it was coming from below. She paused, straining to make out words or determine their exact location.

After a moment of hesitation, she headed for the stairwell.

Adelaide descended two flights, holding onto the railing and the wall for support. The cool metal of the railing anchored her, guiding her fragile steps as she made her way down. The stairwell felt endless, each step a monumental effort in her disoriented state. As she finally exited the stairwell door, she saw Dory crouched by the elevator doors, her flashlight's beam cutting through the darkness.

"Be careful!" Adelaide cried urgently. "Frank's still out there!"

Dory looked up at the voice, her eyes wide with surprise. She took in Adelaide's disheveled appearance.

"Adelaide?" Dory swallowed, her brow furrowing deeply in concern. "What the hell happened to you?"

"It's all my fault!" The confession fell from Adelaide's lips, raw and anguished, as it all rushed out. "The night Oscar disappeared… we were arguing about him and Todd. He was so upset. He ran out, and the elevator doors opened, and he went in without looking! It was an accident… but then Frank… he covered it up. He moved his body!"

Dory waved her off, her expression hardening as she processed this shocking information. "There's no time for that now," she said firmly, focusing solely on the situation. "Frank is behind all this. He's dangerous, and he could be anywhere."

From inside the elevator, Ella's frightened sobs reached their ears. Adelaide's heart clenched with relief and simultaneous dread, her maternal instincts kicking into overdrive.

"Ella, honey," Adelaide called out. "We're here. We're going to get you out of there. Just stay calm, sweetie." She stepped closer to the elevator doors as if her proximity alone could comfort her trapped daughter.

Dory nodded, her expression grim and determined as she returned to the task. Adelaide watched, her hands clasped tightly together, as the detective worked to pry open the elevator doors.

"Ella, listen to me," Dory called out, grunting with effort as she continued to work on the doors. "We're going to get you out of there. Just hold on. Take deep breaths and try to stay as still as possible."

Ella's response was a muffled whimper. Adelaide watched helplessly, her hands trembling as she gripped the railing.

Dory's radio crackled to life, the static-filled voice of her backup team filtering through. "Detective Dingess, we're on our way. ETA two minutes."

The faint sound of wailing sirens in the background grew steadily louder as they approached.

Relief washed over them, but Dory knew they didn't have a moment to spare. She redoubled her efforts to pry open the elevator doors with renewed determination. Her muscles strained against the unyielding metal, pushing with all her might.

Adelaide watched as Dory worked. Her movements were quick and precise. The detective's short, cropped hair was damp with sweat, and her athletic build was tense with effort as she worked to open the elevator doors.

The elevator gave another groan, the sound louder this time. Adelaide's heart leaped into her throat as Dory continued to struggle. The noise reverberated through her very bones, and she silently pleaded for the detective to work faster.

"Almost there, Ella," Dory grunted, her voice strained with exertion. "Just a little more!" She braced her foot against the wall, using it as leverage as she pulled. The doors began to give way, revealing the darkness of the elevator shaft beyond.

Adelaide could see Dory's progress. The metal groaned as it slowly opened, revealing Ella's panicked face.

"Ella, I need you to stay very still, okay? Help is on the way," Dory called out, her voice strained.

Ella's muffled response was filled with terror. She knew they were running out of time, that Frank could be lurking in the shadows, ready to strike again. "Detective, hurry. Frank is still out there."

Heavy footsteps echoed down the hall, the rhythm slow and deliberate. Adelaide instinctively took a step closer to Dory.

Dory's eyes narrowed, her focus unwavering. "Adelaide, go check if that's Frank. I'll keep working on getting Ella out." She paused, meeting her gaze. "Be careful, and if you see him, don't engage. Just come right back here."

Adelaide hesitated for a moment, but the unwavering determination in Dory's voice spurred her into action. She moved cautiously down the hallway, her heart banging in her chest.

She turned down the hallway, her breath caught in her throat. At the far end of the corridor, she saw Frank's imposing figure lumbering towards them. His features were twisted into a scowl, his eyes wild with panic and something darker, more dangerous.

Adelaide's voice was surprisingly calm despite the fear coursing through her veins. "Frank, stop. We know what you did."

Frank's steps faltered, his eyes darting between Adelaide and the elevator where Dory was still working feverishly. A flicker of surprise crossed his features to see Adelaide standing, but he hid the feeling as quickly as it had come.

"You know nothing," Frank snarled. His eyes, cold and hard, bored into Adelaide as he took a threatening step forward. "You have no idea what's going on here. You're hardly even sober," he spat out.

Adelaide stood her ground, her stern face betraying the undercurrent of turmoil she felt inside. Her eyes, sharp and unyielding, locked onto Frank's face as she spoke. "They know about Oscar," she declared, each word carefully enunciated. "They know you covered it up. It's over."

Frank's expression darkened, his hands clenching into fists at his sides. Before he could respond, a loud groan echoed from the old elevator shaft, followed by a piercing screech of machinery.

Adelaide and Frank turned toward the sound, their heated confrontation momentarily forgotten. Dory reached up with both arms, her muscles tense as she pulled Ella safely from the stuck elevator car. Ella's face was pale and streaked with tears, and her clothes were disheveled from the ordeal. In her arms, she clutched Iris.

"Don't take another step!" Dory yelled without missing a beat. She pointed the barrel of her gun directly at Frank. She kept her stance steady, eyes never wavering from her target.

"It's over, Frank. There's nowhere left to run."

Ella's voice was shaky but determined as she found her footing on solid ground; the cat hugged tightly to her chest. "Frank, you can't hurt us anymore! We won't let you."

His eyes flickered rapidly between the three women, darting from Adelaide's stern face to Dory's gun and, finally, to Ella's defiant stance. His resolve visibly crumbled, the fight draining from his body like air from a punctured balloon.

When Dory moved to restrain him, holstering her weapon and pulling out her handcuffs in one fluid motion, he offered no resistance. His rugged features softened in defeat, the lines of anger and hatred melting away to reveal a man broken by the weight of his actions.

Just then, sirens filled the air as backup arrived at the building. The uniformed officers rushed to the scene, their expressions solemn as they took in the situation.

Dory gave a single nod to them, her grip tight on Frank's arm. "I've got this one. Make sure the area is secure."

The officers nodded, moving swiftly to follow her orders. Adelaide watched as they dispersed, a sense of relief heavy in the air.

Ella stepped forward, her eyes fixed on Frank. They were pricked with angry tears. "Why, Frank? Why did you do it? We trusted you. *Oscar* trusted you."

He stared at the floor, unable to meet Ella's accusations. "I knew it was my fault," he admitted, his voice heavy with guilt. "I was responsible for maintaining the elevator. I cut corners. When Oscar... after it happened, I panicked."

"But you covered it up. You let us believe he was missing. Do you have any idea what that did to us?"

Frank's shoulders slumped. "I knew if the truth came out, I'd lose everything. I convinced myself that covering it up was the only way. I wanted to come clean, but I... I was a coward."

"That's enough," Dory cut in firmly. "We'll continue this conversation down at the precinct. You have the right to remain silent, Frank." She allowed the last words to have a bite to them. "I suggest you use it."

Adelaide moved to Ella's side, reaching a bloody handout. She gently squeezed her shoulder. "It's over, Ella. You're safe now."

Dory turned to Ella and Adelaide as she led Frank away, her expression softening slightly. "We'll need to talk about what happened here tonight. But that can wait until morning. Get some rest, both of you. It's been a long night."

Ella nodded, face still haunted by the ordeal. She leaned into her mother's embrace, finding comfort in their usually strained relationship. The weight of the truth settled over them, bringing a strange mix of closure and new grief.

Part Three

Chapter 19

In the days that followed, Oscar's death was ruled accidental, a verdict that brought tumultuous emotions to those who loved him. As his family and friends began the slow, painful healing process, the true impact of Oscar's life became increasingly apparent. His kindness, his laughter, his unwavering love for those around him—these were the things that would endure long after the sharp pain of his loss had faded.

The flickering candlelight danced across the faces of those gathered, casting a warm glow on the memorial that stood before them. Photographs of Oscar adorned the makeshift altar, each capturing a different facet of his vibrant personality. There were snapshots of him as a child, his gap-toothed grin beaming brightly; pictures of him as a teenager, his eyes sparkling with mischief and adventure; and more recent photos showcasing the handsome young man he had become.

A respectful hush fell over the crowd as Ella stepped forward, her eyes shimmering with unshed tears reflecting in the dancing flames.

"Oscar was the brightest light in our lives," she began, her voice shaking with emotion. "He had a way of making everyone feel seen and heard as if they mattered in this world."

Ella paused, taking a deep breath as she scanned the faces of those gathered. Her eyes lingered on familiar features, some etched with grief, others softened by fond memories. "I know many of you have stories to share, memories that capture the essence of who he was," she sniffled. "Tonight, we come together to celebrate his life and honor his impact on each of us."

She gestured to the photos surrounding them, a visual testament to Oscar's vibrant spirit. "In these images, we see the boy who became the man we all loved. But it's in our hearts where his true legacy lives on."

Adelaide followed Ella's lead, her voice choked with emotion as she spoke. "I want you all to know how grateful I am for your support during this difficult time," she said tearfully. "Oscar was more than my son—he was my pride and joy. I promise I will do everything I can to honor his memory."

Todd, with his face pale and drawn, spoke next. His voice wavered slightly as he began but grew stronger as he shared stories of Oscar's infectious laughter, his ability to find joy in the simplest things, and his unwavering loyalty. He recounted anecdotes that brought smiles and tears to the faces of those gathered, painting a vivid picture of a young man who had lived life to the fullest. Todd's eyes occasionally darted to Ella as he spoke, a flicker of something unreadable passing between them.

"Oscar was more than just my boyfriend. He was my soulmate, my other half. He taught me what it means to love unconditionally, to give yourself completely to another person."

As Todd spoke, Peg reached out and took his hand, her eyes shining with tears. She nodded in understanding, her heart aching for the young man who had become her son.

Peg stepped forward and put a comforting hand on Ella's shoulder. "Oscar had a way of making you feel like you mattered like your voice was worth hearing," she said into the microphone, her candle flickering in the gentle breeze. "He was always there with a helping hand, a listening ear, or a joke to lift our spirits. He lives on in the laughter we share, the kindness we show, and the bonds we forge."

One by one, the mourners stepped forward, voices trembling with emotion as they shared their memories of Oscar. A close friend recounted when Oscar threw him a surprise birthday party with all his favorite foods and a personalized cake that made him laugh until tears streamed down his face. A teenager from the apartment below remembered how Oscar taught him to play the guitar, patiently guiding his fingers over the strings until he could strum a tune.

As the vigil continued, each person shared their memories of Oscar. Laughter mingled with tears and stories of adventures and misadventures painted a vivid picture of the young man they all loved. Through their shared grief, a sense of community had been forged, a testament to Oscar's impact on their lives.

Through the event, the pain of his loss, though still there, transformed into a sense of gratitude for having known his soul.

Chapter 20

Ella settled into her window seat on the plane, fixing her gaze on the tarmac outside. Her fingers traced the edge of her boarding pass, the destination written at the top in pretty letters. *London–*. A stark reminder of the life she chose to reclaim.

Her heart thrummed in a steady rhythm, a mixture of anticipation and melancholy inside her as she left behind the familiarity of Bay Ridge, Brooklyn.

The plane began to move, the gentle rocking a prelude to takeoff. She stared out at the world beyond the small oval window, the city below growing smaller and smaller. The familiar skyline of New York gradually faded into the distance, and emotions washed over her—relief, tinged with a bittersweet sense of loss, knowing she was leaving behind the place that had been her home for so long.

She closed her eyes, letting the steady hum of the engines transport her back in time. As the plane soared above the clouds, she felt a sense of hope blossoming within her chest. The road ahead would not be easy. There would be challenges and obstacles to overcome. The weight of Oscar's death would always be there, a shadow in the corners of her heart.

Still, she was determined to make the most of every moment, to honor his memory by living a life that would make him proud.

The pilot's voice eventually crackled over the intercom, informing the travelers that they had reached the halfway point of their transatlantic flight. The seatbelt sign dimmed once again, a soft tone signaling that passengers were permitted to move about the aircraft's interior. Ella unbuckled her seatbelt, eager to stretch her legs and escape the confines of her cramped seat. A sense of relief washed over her as she stood up, her muscles aching from the long hours of sitting motionless.

Around her, other passengers stirred, some reaching into their carry-on bags for books, magazines, or electronic devices to occupy themselves during the lull in the flight. Soft rustles of pages and the occasional beep of electronics filled the air.

Ella made a quick trip to the restroom before a line of other travelers formed, grateful for a moment of privacy and solitude from the crowded cabin.

When she returned to her seat, she pulled out a book she had picked up at the JFK airport newsstand. Sitting, relaxing, and reading for a while was a pleasant change. She found herself quickly engrossed in the story, the words transporting her far from the confines of the airplane. Glancing up, she offered a warm smile to a mother walking down the aisle, cradling a fussy infant. Nearby, Ella noticed the businessman in the next row stretching his legs; his laptop balanced precariously on the tray table as flight attendants moved gracefully through the cabin to offer snacks and drinks to the occupants.

Suddenly, a slight tremor shook the plane, causing the overhead compartments to rattle lightly. She glanced around, noticing a few passengers exchange uneasy looks. She shook it off, attributing it to minor turbulence, and returned to her book.

However, the tremors grew more frequent, each jolt stronger than the last. Ella's grip on her book tightened. She couldn't help but feel a pang of unease. The flight attendants, moving smoothly through the aisles, now seemed more hurried, their expressions tense.

Without warning, a powerful jolt sent Ella and several other passengers flying through the air, their bodies weightless for a terrifying moment. The beverage cart flipped over with a loud crash, spilling a cascade of soda cans and miniature liquor bottles onto the floor. They rolled and bounced down the aisle, adding to the chaos. She cried out in terror as her body slammed against the ceiling with bone-jarring force, the impact shattering the overhead compartment.

Debris rained down in a shower of plastic and metal. Ella felt a searing pain in her shoulder as she was flung back toward the floor, her heart pounding in her chest.

Disoriented and panicked, she struggled to regain her bearings, but the relentless turbulence made it impossible. She reached out, desperately trying to find anything to cling to, but her fingers slipped on the smooth surfaces, sending her tumbling again. The world became a dizzying blur of bright colors and screams.

The plane lurched again with sickening force, and Ella felt a sharp, stabbing pain in her back as she was slammed against the seat in front of her. She cried out, her voice lost amidst the cacophony of screams and the deafening roar of the engines. Her thoughts raced to her family and Sam in London, wondering if she would ever see them again as the aircraft twisted violently through the turbulent sky.

Personal belongings flew—projectiles, books, and laptops scattered across the aisle. Above, more overhead compartments burst open with sickening cracks, showering the cabin with a torrent of jackets, pillows, and bags.

She watched in horror as the woman seated across the aisle was hurled into the ceiling, her head cracking against the unforgiving metal with a sickening thud. Nearby, a man twisted in his seat, his arm bent at an unnatural angle, bone protruding through torn flesh. Loud alarms blared horrendously loud, red lights plunging in and out of service.

Ella's vision blurred, her head spinning from the relentless movements. She saw the woman with the bleeding head slumped in her seat, her eyes vacant, a thin trail of crimson trickling down her pale face. The man with the mangled arm lay groaning on the floor, his cries for help drowned out by the chaos around them.

A warm trickle beaded down her forehead. A piece of debris had struck her. She reached up, her fingers slick with blood as the taste of copper filled her mouth. Her vision blurred further—she fought to maintain consciousness relentlessly, the world tilted on its axis.

Ella closed her eyes once more, her mind drifting back to memories of Oscar, seeking solace in the warmth of his embrace. In her mind's eye, she saw his familiar smile and felt the comforting weight of his arm around her shoulders. For a fleeting moment, the chaos around her faded, replaced by the soothing presence of her twin.

"Oscar, is that really you?"

Oscar's serene face appeared before her, his wide smile as reassuring as it had always been. "Yes, Ella, it's me."

"If I'm with you, does that mean I'm... am I dead?"

Oscar's expression softened. "I don't know," he admitted, "I think you're caught between worlds right now."

Ella looked down and saw her own body lying motionless on the airplane floor. Her heart raced with panic. "What's happening to me? I can't stay here, Oscar. I have to go back."

Oscar squeezed her hand, his touch warm and steady. "I don't know how this works either, but I'm here with you, Ella. You're not alone in this."

Ella's mind raced, torn between the surreal experience of floating between life and death and the grounding presence of her brother. A sense of calm washed over her for a moment, enveloping her in a cocoon of safety.

"Oscar, I've missed you so much. I can't bear the thought of losing you again."

Oscar's eyes filled with love and understanding. "You've never lost me, Ella. I've always been with you in every laugh, every tear, every moment. No matter what happens, that will never change."

A sudden realization hit Ella, and she found a renewed sense of determination. "I need to go back."

Oscar nodded, his smile full of pride. "Yes, you do. You're stronger than you realize, Ella. You've always had that strength inside you."

As the turbulence around her grew more distant, Ella felt herself drawn back towards her body. She clung to Oscar, desperate to hold onto this moment for as long as possible.

"I love you, Oscar," she finally croaked out.

"I love you too, Ella," he replied softly. "Now go. Live your life. I'll always be with you, watching over you."

With that, Ella felt a pulling sensation, and the vision began to fade. The noise and chaos of the airplane cabin rushed back in, but she carried the memory of Oscar's presence with her—a source of strength and comfort that she would bring forward into whatever came next.

Chapter 21

Sam paced the polished hardwood floors of his luxurious London flat, anxiety gnawing at his insides. He paused to straighten a designer throw pillow on the plush leather sofa, his eyes darting to the gleaming stainless steel kitchen appliances. The opulence surrounding him was a glaring reminder of his double life, built on legitimate success and shadowy dealings.

He checked his watch, realizing it was almost time to leave for the hospital. It would be his third visit to Ella's bedside in as many days, a routine that had become both comforting and anxiety-inducing. The doctor's words from their last conversation still rang in his ears: "Ella is stable and healing quickly; it's only a matter of time before she wakes up." The phrase had become a mantra he clung to during the long, quiet hours by her side.

As he grabbed his keys from the marble countertop, he couldn't help but feel a twinge of guilt. The flat, with its high ceilings and panoramic city views, was a testament to his legitimate and otherwise success. His side business of dealing drugs had afforded him this lifestyle, one he was sure Ella would never approve of. The stark juxtaposition between his illicit activities and Ella's pure, unsuspecting nature gnawed at his conscience.

He hesitated at the door, a hand on the polished brass handle. He considered coming clean for a moment, telling Ella everything when she woke up. But the thought of losing her, of seeing disgust in her eyes, was too much to bear. Sam pushed the guilt aside, locking it away in a corner of his mind, determined to keep his two worlds separate.

Taking a deep breath, he stepped out into the hallway, bracing himself for the long hours ahead filled with antiseptic smells, beeping machines, and the growing worry that had become his constant companion. He walked toward the lift, his footsteps clicking on the tiled floor, hoping against hope that today would be the day Ella woke up.

She opened her eyes, greeting the sterile white walls and the comforting hum of machinery. A wave of relief came into her consciousness as she realized she was alive. She could hear the steady beep of monitors and the hiss of oxygen. As her vision came into focus, she stared at the IV lines trailing from her arm.

"Ella? Can you hear me?"

She turned slowly to see Sam sitting in a chair beside her bed; concern etched on his face.

"Sam," she whispered, relieved. "You're here."

Sam's face broke into a genuine smile. "You have no idea how good it is to see you." He brought her hand to his lips, pressing a tender kiss against her knuckles.

"It took everything I've got to get here," she whispered, her words heavy with exhaustion.

They sat silently for a moment, taking comfort in each other's presence. Ella shifted slightly, wincing at the pain in her ribs and back.

"How bad is it?" she asked softly.

Sam's expression softened. "The doctor says you're incredibly fortunate, Ella. You've got some bruised ribs, a concussion, and a sprained wrist, but considering what happened to others on the plane, you've come out relatively unscathed."

Ella's eyes widened. "Oh no. What happened to the others?"

Sam took a deep breath, his face somber. "Many of the survivors... they weren't as well off. Some lost limbs, others may never walk again. The doctor said it's a miracle you escaped with such minor injuries."

Tears welled up in Ella's eyes as the weight of his words sank in. She looked down at her body, still aching but whole, and a sense of overwhelming gratitude washed over her.

"I can't believe it," she whispered. "I remember the turbulence, the screams... I thought for sure that..."

Sam squeezed her hand gently. "You're going to be okay, Ella. The doctor says you'll need some time to recover, but there's no permanent damage. You'll be back on your feet in no time."

Ella nodded, wiping away a tear. The IV tugged painfully at her arm. "How long do I have to stay here?"

"Just a few days for observation," Sam replied. "They want to make sure there are no complications from the concussion. After that, you can come home to recover."

A small smile grew on her face. "Home," she repeated quietly. "Sounds wonderful."

Sam reached into his pocket, his face lighting up. "Speaking of home, someone wants to say hello to you." He pulled out his phone, tapping the screen a few times before turning it towards her.

The video started playing, and her eyes widened as she saw the familiar surroundings of their London flat.

Then, a blur of orange and white fur bounded into view. Ella's heart swelled with emotion.

"Iris," she swooned, her voice catching in her throat.

The cat meowed loudly, her green eyes staring directly into the camera. She padded across the hardwood floor, her tail swishing back and forth as she approached.

"I thought seeing her might cheer you up," Sam said, his voice gentle. "She's been missing you terribly."

Ella watched as Iris gracefully leaped onto the windowsill, her favorite perch for birdwatching. The cat stretched languidly, her paws kneading the air before she settled down, her gaze fixed on something outside the frame, perhaps a fluttering sparrow or a dog out for a walk with its owner.

"She looks so at home," Ella sighed, a mix of joy and longing filling her chest. "I can't wait to see her in person," she added, fingers subconsciously grazing the screen as if she could stroke Iris's fur.

The video continued, offering Ella a glimpse into the cat's daily adventures in the flat. She batted at a dangling toy, pounced on a crumpled piece of paper, and finally, exhausted from her exploits, curled up in a patch of sunlight on Ella's side of the bed. Her contented purr was almost audible through the video feed.

ACKNOWLEDGMENTS

I'm always working on a creative project, usually something related to visual art or music. I enjoy reading so much that I never wanted to dispel that magic by attempting to write a book until one day, the makings of a story began to take shape in my mind, and soon after, I found myself buying and devouring books on storytelling and novel writing. I began working on the book in the winter of 2022, pouring my heart into three drafts, then shelved it in April 2023, waiting for inspiration to strike again.

Life has a way of rearranging our priorities. In December 2023, I lost my mother. In early 2024, I returned to the manuscript to try to find some comfort in my grief and to take my mind off things. I threw myself into the work, rewriting, refining, fixing the outline, and developing the characters. The process was both cathartic and demanding.

As the novel developed, I reached a point where I had written as much as I felt I could on my own. It was time to bring in fresh eyes to review the work and help me see it through to completion. This is where some genuinely talented editors brought their expertise and insight to the book. I'd like to thank Hannah Flood for her developmental edit, Brooke S. for her line editing, and Adeline Hoarau for the copy editing and proofreading.

I'd also like to thank my beta readers, Nova Jarvis, and Mindy Thompson, for their insightful questions and observations, which helped me refine the story further and shape the final product.

Finally, I must express my heartfelt gratitude to my mother for nurturing my love for reading. I'm forever grateful for her influence on this book and my life.

ABOUT THE AUTHOR

Bryce Blackheart, a former phlebotomist who once read avidly between patient blood draws, now channels his passion for books into writing suspenseful thrillers. A longtime New York City resident, Bryce has returned to his roots in Cleveland. *Next Plane to London* is Bryce's debut novel. He now only draws blood on the page.

Milton Keynes UK
Ingram Content Group UK Ltd.
UKHW021903211024
450061UK00012B/154/J